All the Errors

Giorgio Manganelli

All the Errors

Translated from the Italian

by Henry Martin

McPherson & Company

ALL THE ERRORS

Published by McPherson & Company, P.O. Box 1126, Kingston, New York, 12401. Designed by Bruce R. McPherson. Typeset in Bodoni by Delmas Typography. Manufactured in the U.S.A.
1 3 5 7 9 10 8 6 4 2 1990 1991 1992 1993 1994

Library of Congress Cataloging-in-Publication Data

Manganelli, Giorgio.
[Tutti gli errori. English]
All the errors / Giorgio Manganelli : translated from the Italian by Henry Martin.
p. cm.
Translation of: Tutti gli errori.
ISBN 0-929701-07-0 (alk. paper)
ISBN 0-929701-06-2 (pbk. : alk. paper)
1. Manganelli, Giorgio—Translations, English. I. Title.
PQ4873.A48T813 1990
853'.914—dc20 90-5489

This book has been published with assistance from the literature programs of the New York State Council on the Arts and the National Endowment for the Arts, a federal agency.

The paper used in this publication meets the minimum requirements of American National Standard for Information Sciences—Permanence of Paper for Printed Library Materials. ANSI Z39.48-1984.

CONTENTS

All the Errors

Leave-taking

Gentlemen: The condition in which we find ourselves is so precious, dramatic, and rare as to permit me no other desire than to be not entirely unworthy of it. We are about to take leave of one another; more precisely, it is I who am now to advance toward a destiny of which I have no knowledge, and who thus take leave of you with whom, for all I remember, I have always lived. Precisely now, as I continue to be able to recognize and distinguish your faces one by one, and might listen to your voices and speak to you, I know how terrible a privilege my lowly presence here has been, how great a grace the community you have afforded me. I know as well that my banishment is a part of this privilege—indeed its culmination and center of meaning. Nonetheless, while still immersed in this space of light, and still sojourning in this abode of clarity, order, meaning, devotion, and peace, I can only feel both wholly happy, and, beseeching your forgiveness, profoundly sad. I know, and have always known, that this has a place in our pact; and I likewise know that the selfsame experience I refer to as unhappiness is in itself a great and demanding and propitious revelation. Yet how greatly I recoil, nonetheless, from deserting the home of my being, our congress, to confront, then, what must, by definition, contract, your deliberation, and my choice, be unknown.

I do not intend to thank you, since no gratitude of mine can reach up to you, unless as an act of unwarranted familiarity. But I call attention to the clarity, peace, and sanity I have known, how great and decisive they have been. Now I am to lose all of it. No, you have not withdrawn, nor signalled yet for my own departure. Though you continue to lodge within your perfect, habitual silence, I know you to give your inward assent to my words as you listen to me; and that you understand me, even if your understanding precludes any exemption from the task that confronts me. As I speak I know myself to consume irreplaceable instants that will never be returned to me, and thus am fully aware that anything I say, no matter what, can only be miserly, feeble, and cowardly, even if it kernels still intact the most perfect devotion of love. With quiet anxiety I contemplate the clarity of your faces, knowing with what imminence they will start to darken and waver, and finally vanish. For now, I anchor myself again into the merciful coherency of your profiles, and again take the measure of lineaments which for me were eternal; I know that I remain, for an ever more fragile fraction of time, still with you, within your protection and government.

I can focus, as I speak, on the slow, constant swelling of a fear that now resides inside me; something obscure and heretofore unknown has begun to coalesce in my interior. It slowly grows. There continue to be ways in which I can dally, yet I know that my dalliance, no matter how protracted, is destined to finish. I now experience an actual adumbration of that end of which all my previous notions have been solely and entirely mental. Now I truly know that my sojourn within this dwelling-place has begun to approach its conclusion.

In these slow and perfect moments—their perfection unmarred by their anguish—I discern new feelings as they enfold themselves among those I have already professed to you: I know, gentlemen, that I am destined to lose peace, order, meaning, honor, and love. I savor this still intact and ever-enduring peace and hug it once more against me, even while not only knowing, but actually discerning that it starts to abandon me. I have now a direct and tactile sensation of the closeness of fear, disorder, dishonor, and lovelessness. And yet I would tell a lie if I made the assertion that this, as it slowly rises, is the greatest anxiety that consumes me. I fear and suffer the quakings of distress, and the affliction of lovelessness, but still I am here with you. Even if somehow more apart than I have ever been before, nonetheless I can recognize you, one by one, and might speak to you; and should you address your words to me, I could listen, assent, and obey. This dwelling is not what it will later be: I shall come to see it as extraneity itself, the place of which nothing can ever be known, and perhaps as the very seat of fear and persecution. Nothing in the undeniable veracity of what I suffer now, still here before you, can strike me as kindred to the future suffering that awaits me, of which the anguish, the dimensions, and the horror know no confines, gentlemen, no comparison. Because, gentlemen, I shall forget you, and this abode, and your light. I will first forget your profiles, and your names; and though a dazed but never to be doubted recollection of this dwelling and of those who govern it will perhaps for a while endure, even that mindfulness of a taciturn light will soon commence to dissolve, strain as I may to fix it into knowledge. But my forgetfulness will grow complete: not only, gentlemen, of your profiles, nor only of this abode and your light, but even of the fact that such profiles and luminous places exist. I shall remember nothing at all. Finally I will not suspect, nor believe to know, but shall truly know that you do not exist and have never existed. I shall perceive you to be nothingness. In an alternation of pride and horror, I will know the government of every existent thing to belong to dishonor and lovelessness.

Perhaps I will suppose that you exist, a fantasy of the mind, entrusted perhaps to dreams, cabals, and recurrent numbers. You are the lords of clarity and love, and I shall hate you and fear you, and flee before the terror that you may possibly spy me out; and if I think of your dwelling, I shall imagine it a place of obscurity and pain. But more than anything else, with passing time, what will be most probable is this: that I shall cease to think of you at all and consider you either blandly inimical or simply void. You will have no profiles, there will be no abode, no light, and the world I live in—as now I live in this one—will be finally a globe of shadows, of desert, and totally absent of meaning. If I have children I will faithlessly teach them to fear and abhor this place as a place of torture, and I will teach them to think of you as evil, creatures full of ire, images of unimaginable filth. I will know rain, snow, sickness, the love of the flesh, betrayal of self and of others, mendacity, rage, fear, flight, hunger, rancor and irreparable solitude that can know no balm, cut off from that sole medication which is everything now here in this abode. I will search for the narrow path between despair and no hope, and attempt my suicide, holding in check both my hate and my love for what will then be able to be no more than a fantasy of this abode. I will live through years unworthy of being lived, and as age sets in to force me towards my termination, I will begin, you see, to be afraid. In my cowardice, I shall raise questions about the existence of your profiles, about the possibility and nature of this dwelling-place, about this light and how, if you exist, you will greet and take me in. I will alternate attempts to prove you nonexistent with hopes that will fill me with the fear that you exist. I shall be horrified by nothingness, and terrified of you. At night I shall lie awake, I who can still now see you, and I will litter the darkness with questions. I shall look for ghosts of creatures uselessly loved that I have lost, and when I see them they will frighten me, and I will spurn and deny them. The journey that is now to begin, gentlemen, will have precisely this as its paramount and guiding purpose: to deny you, and to think of you as void or criminal. And then, when mortality will finally have found its moment of inevitability, the whole spool of error so inextricably entangled as no longer to beg for ungarbling, but instead to be destroyed, I suppose I will once again be shown toward this abode, but lacking all ability, gentlemen, to recognize you in any way at all. The pupil you have known as a loved and obedient acolyte will reappear before you as a shadowy phantom of fear, revulsion, despair, and self-loathing, expectant of catastrophe. My once gentle visage will be a specter of rot; and you will find a horror in the sight of something that will strike you as not unknown, yet hardly as identifiable; something moreover that will lack all desire to be identified. And your light will blind me, and reveal my belabored and limitless ugliness, that thing I for too many years will have spoken of as "I."

Your profiles will be objects of my ignorance, and your names will be infamy to infamous ears; finally again we will stand as close to one another as now, yet irreparably extraneous, separate, and lost.

I have no notion of what will happen in that solemn, terrific moment when you, intact as you are now intact, will newly meet me, deformed by a life that I will not have known how not to have lived. You send me, gentlemen, into life in order that I bring this back to you, here within your perfect dwelling-place. I am to return with darkness, fear, ignorance, and despair. Because just as I now and will always thirst and hunger for your placid immensity, perhaps a lust lies hidden in you to know, and here in this abode to hold in custody what you cannot otherwise acquire than through my dispatch. I will return as evil, as unbalmable pain, as blemish; and even, with time, if I learn again to recognize your profiles, I will see them no longer as I see them now, in this moment of taking leave of you, but rather as obscurely thoughtful, shrouded within the pain of an incomprehensible silence; and this light will be different, as different as my ineradicable shadow will be able to render it, the shadow that accompanied me throughout a life. This, gentlemen, is not only the final moment in which I shall know you and you shall know me. This is the final moment of our love. From the start of my life, you will be unsoundable and secret anguish; and starting from my death, I will stand newly before you, but reciprocally unknown and incomprehensible: I forever governed by fear, and you by the tender horror that can only be aroused by something torn and deformed, and that could not have been saved, nor at all exempted from its task of existing. Gentlemen, the clamor now roaring at my shoulders has made me deaf; for the first time my eyes experience darkness; I bid farewell, and fall, and lose you, and am born.

Lovers

What ties me to this man is the uselessness, or what I can better describe as the constant pain of our relationship, his having lodged himself in my existence as a thing that both defrauds and simulates life, and that relieves me from the effort, for me the utterly uncongenial effort of living. Though I have tried to despise him, or to plumb the tedium of his alloy of insolence and defeat, I have never proved capable of quite so much: to hate him would mean reobtaining a license for living, which I find repugnant. But still I think I would have to call myself a liar if I asserted what ties me to this man is love, even a debased and inferior form of love. I find something astonishing here: that a sign or an empty but recognizable imprint always remains in the place in the soul where a love—even the faultiest love—was once at work, something like the plaster of paris cast hardened on the sharpened features of a corpse. That mask is empty yet marks the locus of love, and so I admit to experiencing love as absence and void, or a cold silhouette that hides inside me like a child refusing to be born. Old, habitual gestures sometimes reappear on the rare occasions when we meet, but their return disconcerts both of us like sudden, unsummoned evidence that something once truly happened between us, and that something else still bears it distracted but truthful witness. Great gaps lie between our discourses, and continued discourse is something we have surely abandoned; but sometimes we offer ourselves the cheer of some rapid sequence of images, some allusion that re-establishes us as accomplices. I say "cheer" since our sufferings, which are certainly known to the both of us in spite of how different they are, will find themselves veiled with the rag of a kind of modesty, a zone or winding sheet of ephemeral hilarity. This cheer then finds itself succeeded by a deeper and separate bitterness which it is not within our power to share: a harsh, disoriented feeling and an act of recognition through a ritual of farewells, which nonetheless has a gift of perverse exactitude in its reconstruction of the scheme, or should I say the skeleton, of a life that would even be coherent if only I would adapt myself to this grating task of being alive, the use of myself for living. I have no idea whether this thing I call a tie is withering away day by day, consuming itself in ever lengthening silences, or whether it has achieved some mode both of being and not being, circumscribing a place where nothing more can happen. Both of us are insects caught in amber, yet in some way or another undead, even if something precludes us from entertaining a relationship with what the living call life. Because our story has not been brief, it will sometimes happen that I search out memories, and I am amazed to see that even our past has accommodated itself to the destiny of this amorous default of love in the present. It too has become an insect, a minuscule animal of which I study the legs and the wings with slight disgust, a tenderness that never fails to revolt me and which my body, with tenderness as always, perceives in its interior like a pair of tongs. And do I not sometimes address him with affectionate words, as if within me such words were licit? But since everything within me is illicit, yet tolerated, even if intolerable, I do not disapprove of myself. The objects I handle show the poorness of intrinsic poverty, and they hide me. It is possible even that I am grateful to him for this hiding place, this refuge like an arm bent back across my eyes, shielding them from the sun.

What ties me to this woman is the slowness, the inertia, the lack of meaning in the whole of my life. Among all the artful defeats I have managed to live, it is this one, perhaps, this history of so many years, that achieves perfection. Perfection in its irony, its implications, its overdeterminations and allusions. And how would it be if what I call defeat held the very imprint of my life? I know that love is over and done with, but I also know that there is never, strangely enough, an end to what is truest, most pertinent, and most affecting about love, which is its pain. It's said that jealousy outlives love, but I am certain that jealousy too is outlived by pain. When we have struggled to wrench so much from life and nothing remains but this filthy, crystalline residue of suffering, an allusive ideological suffering, this suffering becomes something we refuse to relinquish, simply out of egotism. How can a story be so long, and yet so brief in memory? How can the condition of "being dead" occupy the very same space as the whole of a life? I know that she feels neither esteem for me, nor enmity: yet in a way she both holds me in disesteem and knows nothing at all about me, even though I continually touch her life, as she can't help touching mine—touching one another with an always implicit "Sorry." I am entirely aware that the place we separately inhabit is first of all painful: and yet we are separately tied to this poor, meagre pain, this docile desperation that still permits us a kind of familiarity somewhere between the despicable, the impatient, and in its own way noble—almost like people in reciprocal vigil during an epidemic. No, an epidemic won't do: here there is no surrounding fear, but simply the constant presence of a witness, an accountant among catalogs who presides over the times and places when we meet. Both of us by now are incapable of heat, but this nothingness, this cold, is something we understand more intimately than anybody else; and in our own particular way, though with irony, we think of ourselves as experts, even if we make no further claims on the rough-shod friendship of experience.

What ties me to this man is a catalog of things of slight account, precisely in the sense that they could be neither bought nor sold, and there is no attic in which to store them; things that bear a whiff of shame, which is a feeling I love. If I examine my life and his life, these two lives that form no arithmetic sum, shame is the acutest sign I see, the blazon and trademark. This is what led us to believe we loved each other, but shame was our constant companion. Wasn't it then that we decided, unawares, that we ourselves would somehow be vehicles of shame? Shame revolved around us, and now it stands again where it stood at the start, directly in front of us, an habitual mirror.

What ties me to this woman is the point to which she led my life: her pitiless sweetness, that derangement of roots. Thanks to her I made the acquaintance of perdition, but not the generous, fantastic perdition of love. Perdition pure and simple, the lacerated tunic of an ill-shaped body. And there you have it: I am tied to this woman by my deformity, since without her I would never have discovered myself to be deformed. I want to be deformed, but don't believe that any way more pertinent than love can so summon an oriental grace into the limning of a cripple's sores, wrinkles, and paralytic subtleties. When I speak of perdition pure and simple, I know of no explications to offer, unless tautologically. Perdition is to lose oneself, and to lose oneself is to be lost. An object lost on a street that no one walks. An object left out in the sun, to the night, to the frost, for the dogs, for the end of the world. But something else as well: a creature ignorant of his own face, lost in the wilds, in a labyrinth, in a trap-work of valleys; astray in a building that belongs to him, but of which no one has ever given him the map, and moreover where no one has ever lived, if not the lost man himself. I rarely encounter that woman, but every time I do I experience the enthralled and delighted degradation of the animal that was mortally wounded, and since then irreparably lamed. So when I speak of something that "ties me" to this woman, my language is correct while remaining inappropriate: I would be tied to this woman even if I were never to see her, and our entanglement is in any case no property of our rare and quiet meetings. I know that this woman has forgotten nothing, but I know as well that my body's mangledness is the most precious and astute of the memories she preserves; and she is not in the wrong, and I am grateful for it. It was she who brought this fatal deformity to light, subtracting it from the order of mendacity that eclipsed it. Discovering my deformedness she also discovered her own; and though we no longer speak so much as a word of it, both of us recognize and with secret tears of abandon we piously fondle the monstrous reciprocal coherency that we alone are to comprehend.

What ties me to that woman is the fact, the very probable fact, that after having loved me she entirely ceased to love me, but deciding as well, from out of her natural kindliness, to hold me afloat in a fluid of questions which, if I weren't the vile creature I by now have discovered myself to be, I hardly ought even to risk referring to as questions. I can maintain that my revealing myself to be totally vile is among the gifts this woman has lavished: my having discerned my task as illusionless waiting while adorning the life of another with my poverty, and more than all else while tasting the difficult savour of "almost-non-being"—a condition I discover not only to be congenial but even salubrious in its own particular way. I have to add, straitened as I am by lovelessness into loveless dependency, that I am as though perpetually busied with chores of trifling significance, like a clerk continually diverted from work not entirely devoid of importance, however lowly, and reassigned to tasks that are absolutely null: moving an empty inkwell, emptying an ashtray, straightening a slightly crooked sign that reads "No Entrance." These risible and slightly despicable chores may perhaps have been meted out with intentions of secret ridicule, but they can just as possibly be free of even so much as a trace of contempt, my inborn loathesomeness having summoned them up. Here, however, I see I have shifted from the theme I had most at heart: these "chores" that descend from this senseless, finally painless dependency—discounting the utterly gratuitous pains to be borne in the servitude of a poor if not ignoble soul—these chores, I say, hold me at a distance from the splinterings of a love life, which I'd in no way be able to bear. So I won't deny that this naked, inert, and passive life I lead somehow preserves, protects, and companions me. It is possible that this love story, which is what I like to call it even if it isn't a story and accommodates no love, will always remain inconclusive; that it will never reach the ireful, noble moment of an explanation. I myself, in fact, am neither ireful nor noble, and this woman I love, or rather by now, in truth, dislove, has no passion for being proud and clear, nor indeed for any form of pride and clarity. No, she isn't cruel, just as I myself am not demanding, not in any way. I am certain other men have known her, between one telephone call and the next, and I myself, moreover, have known more than one other woman. But I hope the essential thing isn't slipping from view. The essential thing is that I am distracted by these chores, and thereby deflected from loving; and that our indulgence in a similarly ambiguous situation, ambiguous by convention alone, confers a delicate bouquet of transgression to the carnal acts she doubtless performs, making her culpable and adulterous, never releasing her from me and my tiresome presence, which is just as much an absence. So I too give her a gift of something that strikes me as essential to her image of herself: a kind of soft guiltiness that perplexes her and makes her body graceful, that body which has a beauty that corresponds to no interior strength. Here I have used a word I rarely use, and which perhaps I ought to explain: this woman is strengthless, just as I myself have no strength. We are tied together by a missing destiny, and our movements are random, provisional, and uninformed by meaning. I make no complaint, but cannot help realizing that this, in fact, is what most fundamentally binds us: the lack of a destiny. I like to think back to the days when this woman would concede herself to me, if I can allow myself this no longer current verb, but only because her having ceased to concede herself allows me to savor my "almost-not-being" as a distinguishing trait of my life, a special feature to be noted on my passport. I am certain too that she thinks back to those days as well, and perhaps that memory fires her. But fires her to what? Both of us know that we are reciprocally lost, and we know that fire has nothing to do with us. Loving each other, if we ever did, was a less than forthright way of pretending to be immortal. Do you see what I mean? But now that we have returned to the peace of our decadence, to the senseless labyrinths of our days, to games of dice and cards with no ante at stake, no one would dare any longer to talk about love. But it's precisely because our labyrinths are deconsecrated—places fit for the reek of the urine of dogs—that she persists and I agree to persist in this game, this counterfeit torture, this infinite protraction of a fictive love and its simulated anticipation of a clarification of something of untold importance, the pretence that it will soon itself be a turning point where everything changes and immortality starts over once again. All of this is a lie, naturally enough, and what will happen is that I will be asked to empty the waste paper basket. Can I say that I am unhappy? No, I can't. In a way, I have enjoyed the rare and stupendous revelation of knowing myself for what I am, a creature designed from the start to be the very least of things, and who has always been faithful to that condition, finally to the point of having made a style from my obedience to nullity, and a destiny from my lack of destiny.

What ties me to that man is how he apprises me of the humiliation of existence: without this bond I would never have quickened to the humiliation in having been born, in having a body, in being capable of desire, in the anxious need to feel myself desired, in love. By myself I might see such things to shape a revelation of a strange and overwhelming beauty; for example, that falling in love is a scroll consigned to me by some magic fowl, perhaps by the Holy Ghost, in order to give meaning to my life.

But the experience of humiliation in such of its guises as I have actually experienced is to know that in the body, in love, in desire, and in falling in love, there lies enclosed an incorruptible center of defeat which is the irreparable meaning of everything that happens to me, and which I would never hope to repair. The man to whom I am bound does not humiliate me; to the contrary, he is kind and meek; but he bears the marvelous and unmistakable odor of defeat. No, he is not ill; nor is he a man who would be capable of disloyalty; and I imagine him to be faithful, since fidelity is a part of this humiliation. He has no craziness, and only a few innocent manias, like the way he will endlessly rub his hands together, as though warming them, never saying a word; or there's a movement he makes with his left shoulder, less even that a nervous tick, almost a timid allusion to some threat not really to be taken seriously. I grow aware of how difficult it is to explain what I mean by humiliation, since even falling in love, which I have experienced, is exempt from any meaningful definition. I will put it like this: the man to whom I am tied "doesn't happen." He exists, works, makes money, and eats; he's taciturn, but without impoliteness; he's healthy, he's patient, he's affectionate, but nothing could make him "happen." I could explain it like this: rather than his occupying space, it is space that steps aside from all around him; I don't intend to say that space feels any anger towards him, simply that space recognizes him as extraneous. That's the word: he's extraneous, not alien, not monstrous, but simply an object set up in the wrong place; a flashlight in a lost, wrecked, dilapidated suitcase. Perhaps there's a light in this man, but it is hidden so deep down, and his body is so arranged that even he has lost all awareness of it. He is closed up inside of this tract of the world; closed up in a drawer, closed up in a wardrobe, closed up in a pick-up truck. Since I am tied to him, I have accepted having to look into that drawer, to dust off that wardrobe, to travel in that pick-up truck, since, absurdly enough, that pick-up truck runs. I have accepted: but really I could not have done otherwise. This is what my vocation has always been: the humiliation that grows from contiguity to something that is absolutely central but which never happens. In this way, the place, the space, the locus inhabited by this man to whom I say I'm tied appears to me increasingly, every day, to be an impossible place, because that place is simultaneously occupied—just as a hat "occupies" a space—deserted, and yet again central. Which of these characteristics in itself is central, I do not know; but certainly not centrality. Still, in this unheard-of poverty of existence, this penury I stubbornly refer to as love, as a tie, as falling in love, as living together, in this allegorical machine both great and terribly anguishing—no, not anguishing but rudimentary and senseless—in this ceremony of caricature and atheism, this method of being totally crushed by the awareness of the fact of existing, there is yet a meaningless meaning that has nothing grand or heroic about it, coalescing with humiliation into a single thing. It is clear that any woman traveling in a pick-up truck along with a wardrobe containing a drawer inhabited by a man who does not "happen" will frequently have the impression of being alone, and of being in the grip of some innocuous dementia; but what, with a certain literary artifice, I have now spoken of "innocuous dementia" is in reality the selfsame thing as humiliation. After all, the man who I say "does not happen" might conceivably be non-existent; he might simply be a hole that space has chosen not to fill; but in that case his significance would be enormous, he would be nothing less than "the center." So are humiliation and the center the very same thing? I look at my body and imagine how happy I would be if the conditions of "not happening," humiliation, and extraneousness were the definition of the center; and that I, alone, like a child having fled from herself, should have plumbed to such a depth, arriving so close to everything, even though deprived of being, that is.

What ties me to that man is the impossibility of capturing him, of stopping him, of interposing my body in the midst of the route between him and his destruction; since there is no doubt that he is slowly destroying himself. In this sense, this man to whom I am tied possesses something rare, precious, and exceptional; he proceeds, totally unaware, toward an objective, his life has an itinerary, even if I wouldn't be so bold as to say it has a destiny. For years, I tried to re-route him from his patient, meek disintegration; but on a day of singular placidity I understood that desperation is hope's companion, and I ceased both to hope and to suffer. I broached no further arguments, I tabled no further discussions of the minute contradictions in his behavior, his talk, his thinking. I have ever more frequently assented; I avoided questions I ever less wanted to ask, and to which I attributed an ever lessening importance—questions, in any case, that he would forget. More than death, the theme of this man's life is disintegration. No longer acting, doing nothing to save him—as though some form of salvation might exist—I only observe him. Yet the gesture he might perform to save himself strikes me as obvious, banal, and limpid; to save himself and bring about the day by day regression of that monstrous collapse in which I believe he finds self-recognition, and for which he in any case doesn't know how to propose an alternative, nor even to conceive of one, none at all. For years I thought: "It would take so little." But now I understand that precisely this "so little" gives dignity to his crumbling: decadence is a part of his nature, and not even the incumbency of the most minimal gesture would tempt him towards salvation. He speaks little, and ever less; his words are sometimes confused, but not rarely enjoy an ephemeral clarity. I no longer take either joy or pain, but accept a kind of mute complicity in it; by now I do not want the reversal of his disintegration; and even if I have no desire to hasten it, I have decided that this space of decay—an ever more unstable and straiter space—is precisely the locus of our appointment. In his own way, I believe that he has never stopped loving me, even if what I call love is in him something strange, more resembling a large rat than an emotion: a thing with a life of its own, and that has dug out a nest among debris—among that debris which still bears his name. For some time now, he has taken no interest in the world, in what takes place outside our house; but within this house, the place where I exist and he exists, he shows a state of acute and perhaps frightened interest, a mixture of horror, uneasiness, predilection and protection, an alternation of desperation and tenderness. He's intrigued by the chairs; the wall clock alarms him; the creaking of the doors perhaps presents him a message that he does not interpret, yet that does not escape him. Finally there is me. Every morning, my presence is the object of a bland stupor, which makes me think his interior sense of time has been demolished, and that always he has the impression of once again rebeginning the very same day. Sometimes I see him perform gestures as though fearing to get them wrong, as though he were running the danger of an action that might plummet him into a day where he'd find no orientation. I imagine him to think, "If I get into a different day, will she be there?"

And so the days transform themselves into a single day, and we are every day certain of encountering one another; and he shows a kind of gratitude, not directed to me as a person, but for my presence, as a guarantee that nothing has happened. In reality, this very guarantee I offer him seems little by little but uninterruptedly to favor his disintegration, and through my tacit agreement to provide this guarantee I become its accomplice. But I have no other way of remaining in his company; I have no other way of living a life in which I am I and he is "you." Certainly, nothing could be easier for me than to leave this house forever and blank out all knowledge of what will become of him. And if I stay here, it is not out of charity, and not out of love. Perhaps I've been fascinated by the way the days repeat themselves; or by his intense, attentive fear of the future, that ability to live literally without a future in a caricature of eternity. I have grown fond of the constantly growing squalor of his existence, and I find it congenial, especially for the blithe, distracted method with which he lives in that squalor. I imagine him to live in a circular world where everything is strangely homogeneous, with neither entrances nor exits. And I am admitted into this circular room without his knowing it, since I too have begun to relish this daily horror of the future. No, I don't believe that any such collapse as takes place in him has begun to take place in me: that would be beyond me. I will always attempt that minimal gesture, and I'll attempt, ignobly, to save myself. I taste the shadows that he tenders with his trembling hands, and I receive them into my own, not without thankfulness. I am a living creature that goes to him every day, every hour, for its ration of darkness. As things by now have come to stand, I would find it insipid to live without that darkness, and I too spurn the future. Perhaps his collapse will one day become precipitous, and he will slip into the heart of his shadows. But I am wise and foresightful, and always on my guard; because when that moment comes, I shall be quick to rip from his hands all the remaining darkness they contain, and I will make it last me for the whole of the life—a life of "todays"—that still remains to me.

What ties me to this woman is her total, devastating defeat. She was, and still is, a woman of interesting emotions: a quick, amiable, sometimes chattery woman, never threatening. There were moments when I found her extraordinary; and as such, I was afraid of her; but now I know that her beauty, her kindness, and the daring of her finely conceived projects conceal complete defeat. In reality, and paradoxically, what binds me to her is something that ought to hold me at a distance: the fact that she has never left me, as everything in her demanded. And even though I know she has betrayed me, and experienced the first sketches of passions, she has never managed to leave me, even with my knowing that she does not love me, just as I must confess that I do not love her. Yet all the same, at this point in our story, both of us, defeated and equal witness to the defeat of the other, have become indispensable to one another in some delicate and abject way. As one day followed another, her beauty became first useless, and then a symptom; a kind of delusion on the part of the body, a delusion of grandeur, to which nothing about her was in any way adequate. She is a tender woman, an extremely tender woman, even though I know that she is infatuated only with her tenderness itself and never by its object. But I know still more: I know it to be only in me that she can find an object so laboriously defeated as to generate this savage, demented love for her own tenderness. Now she no longer has plans, neither of us any longer has plans;

she is content with simply denying assent to a pretence that would force her exit from her patiently constructed dementia. I'd like someone to listen to our talks, which are frequently long, since both of us like to talk, deploy concepts, and then forget. But this isn't what I wanted to deal with, which is instead our reciprocal solicitude and gentleness, our hastening to admit that the other is right, our mixture of assent, cowardice, and complicity, even of gaiety, as though we'd both had a marvelous idea in choosing to live such a delicate, finely-crafted, and elegant defeat. All around her, and thus around me as well, a story of an elegance listing toward madness has established itself; just the barest hint of a list, since this elegance never ceases to be elegance, and is slightly demented only in how she so clearly flaunts it, and I along with her, in the face of emptiness. We eat delicate foods, we go to plays, we read books, always in the selfsame way, by twos, together, and we smile a great deal. She knows that I will never reprove her for her adulteries, and that I will never exit from her life. Each of us is an expert in the defeat and elegant sickness of the other: we'd truly be incapable of separation. Yes, there is too much gentility; and sometimes she is afraid of it, as am I. We have nightmares, each of us screaming alone. We give each other pendants of real tears, scattered everywhere by our cunning voidance of love.

What ties me to this woman is her perfect capacity to mislay me, like some precious object marbled with bitter memories. I am not a continuous presence in her life, but an image balanced on her shoulder, a fowl she every now and then will shoo away with a nonchalant gesture. This impermanence of love in a woman who has become the central hieroglyph of my life is an essential part of that hieroglyph. Without this vocation for the loss of ourselves, I can no longer understand me. I know the eyes of this woman in the moments when she loves me, if the word is apt, or at any rate in the moments when I am counted among the objects she catalogs as parts of her life. Such eyes are clear, quiet, and attentive. Attentive more than anything else. For a few days, a few hours, I delude myself, I delude myself every time, that that calm, that uncreased obstinacy, might strike roots, that I might find a definitive home in those eyes, that the inventory of her life might never in any moment be ever again manipulated. Because I cannot manage to subtract myself from the impression, the entirely fabulous impression, that this woman is the object of a manipulation: not any deliberate, calculated sorcery on the part of any single individual, but an anonymous, secret, and yet utterly manifest spell that might have been woven by a rock, a plant, or a change of the wind. My hope that those eyes will continue to look at me as they do, that the spell will no longer be able to act, and that I myself may prove to be adequate repair against so astute an invasion is of course an entirely desperate hope, with no foundation; and yet it always returns, and always with the air of something new, potent, persuasive, and intimately logical. Then the spell asserts itself. I see those eyes lose their hold on things, among which things I myself have been placed; the fowl on her shoulder is shooed away with some bland, distracted gesture that's fully unaware of what it brings about. Her eyes rise free from the illusion of their rootedness, and their imprecise-ness becomes ungraspable. I know that, once again, she has mislaid me. I have learned not to suffer intolerably during such hours, which might every time be final, and I have even mastered the possibility of holding the figure of being mislaid within the more general design of my existence. Her mislaying me has become a part of my own way of mislaying me; if I am not on the shelves of her world, I am nowhere at all; I become as vague as a speck of sterile pollen, an object so light that every wind will carry it wherever it chooses. When expelled from those shelves, I truly have no place to go. I waver in the midst of the air like a phantom forgetful of the formula that governs its voyages and its rendezvous with the living. This condition of being a creature of flux has by now grown dear to me, and perhaps I no longer dare to relinquish it. But I don't really mean to say that my most profound condition is prevalently dependent upon how I deposit myself in this woman's interior spaces; I am saying, rather, that my having "been mislaid" is a quality inherently my own; a vocation; a frail but not secondary form of destiny. It is necessary that I be mislaid, that I wander in a personal wood, that the house be denied to me, that I come finally to nurture doubts about my name, and that all possible roads become at a certain point equal, even though I in no way feel myself lost. This availability to an erratic, imprecise, and destitute, but in its own way imaginative existence is something I wouldn't know how to deny myself; my depths possess a touch, and something more than a touch, of the vagrant, the mendicant, the bum who sleeps beneath bridges. The vagrant, in the sense I now apply to the word, is the person with no shelves, seats, or locus in which to deposit himself; someone whose name is known only to a few, and largely by chance and imprecisely; a being less bizarre than extravagant: extra-vagant, wandering through some outside. During these hours when I have been mislaid, I experience lilliputian feelings, impoverished affections, desertified places, fleeting and unstable images. I live among creatures whose existence as a rule is unknown to me and that perhaps do not exist except in the moments when I accept to be mislaid. I too live myself as a minuscule image that can find its home in the joinings of old, rotted furniture, and the longer my being mislaid endures, the longer I travel within my diminutive geography, in seas the size of a fingernail, then of a grain of rice, then the point of a pin. My interior voice is the chirp of a minute animal that knows neither how to fly, nor to swim, nor to run; and if I remember the bird perched on her shoulder, I have no doubt that a part, carefully choosing that word, yes, that a part of that bird that was really more dismissed than anything I'd hazard describing as having been driven away, there having been no intention to offend, a part of that winged thing is a part of me, and perhaps that part, in its obstinate experience of miniature seas, which never ceases to remember the greater seas of her shoulder. There might even, perhaps, be no lack of precision in maintaining that I myself, and I alone, am involved in the manipulation of that spell that demands that she mislay me. Yet as I write the word "involved," I understand it to be true that this spell would surely be impossible without me, but no less true that I am but one of its ingredients, albeit an essential ingredient. During my vagabondage as a mislaid thing through always more impervious places, unintelligible and unknowing, I grow aware of nothing like nostalgia, but of a modification of the hieroglyph that informs the whole of my life. I know the woman to whom I am bonded to have issued from the depths of her sleep, which is a singular sleep that concerns no one but me, me alone. The supple rootings of her slightly disquieted gaze search me out in the spaces I now inhabit; I feel myself cautiously sought, tracked down like a vagrant on the brink of death and to whom a message that will totally alter his condition is now, with all due caution, to be communicated: he is no longer to be a vagrant and his demise is to be postponed, perhaps indefinitely. I feel someone on the roam within this wood of the thousand pathways, and I perceive that something inherent to any such exploration must be spoken of as courage, since this wood is not the natural habitat for whomever seeks me out, as it is to me. Womanly fingers which I know quite well become miniature so as to be able to touch me without doing me injury, to recognize me. Finally, a cautious voice sounds down to that bottom I have reached and exerts itself upon me like a wind, a bizarre, sucking wind that calls me once again to stand before those eyes that have newly found me. Suddenly, furiously, I abandon my minuscule places and minimal seas, my ephemeral images. I relinquish everything, and not without a sense of loss, feeling myself as though called upon to float between two different modalities of loss. Finally, when I discover myself reshelved in the well-defined spaces of this woman to whom I recognize myself to be tied, I recognize as well that that previous site, the site just now relinquished by the no-longer mislaid me, is just, opportune, and endowed with meaning. Oh, not a wholeness of meaning, and yet a large if not entirely essential portion of meaning. Those eyes then scrutinize and question me, perhaps with apprehension, almost aware that both of us have mislaid ourselves and one another. Moments of a strange, exacting, captious tenderness intermingle with instants of affectionate diffidence. Something both definitive and conditional rebegins. Deeply articulated roots again re-form, and yet the earth into which they strike is, as always, a sandy earth, courted by wind, sun, and emptiness. I surprise myself with desiring that this mislaying be the last; and I believe that there is fear in the eyes that seek me out, fear that I could come to be mislaid to the point of never again being findable, a definitive inhabitant of my invisible seas. In that moment, we stay close to one another, but cautiously, almost fearing we could frighten one another; and then I capitulate to the magisterial sway of those eyes, the fowl settles on the shoulder, once again there rebegins the long, subtle, taciturn conversation of pupils, and eye-lashes, and eyes of a candor that reminds me of the expanses I have abandoned and to which I will be returned, no less placid than overwrought, by the signs of the next, inevitable moment of being again mislaid. Now I am grateful to that gaze; I accept the having of a place; my name is firmly established; and once again, both jejune and astute, I begin to hope.

What ties me to that woman, briefly, is that she does not exist; no, I don't mean to say that she doesn't exist at all or is only the product of my fantasy, an hallucination, a delirium, a madness; as far as existence is concerned, she exists; she has a body, she has the use of words, she has hair. It's for me, as I think about her here, that she has no existence; she no longer has thoughts, and I couldn't say since when. Yet I could meet the need to prove that woman's existence by recalling the story that actually, if I again make no mistake, took place between us, which is a story utterly similar to the stories that get told in books, and which old men remember not without tenderness. Telling that story, moreover, if I wish, I could also remember a host of minute particulars; but really I couldn't care less. It's enough to be certain I haven't gone mad, and to prove it to myself that this woman exists—and now I say "this woman," though really for no reason—even, as I've already said, if she has no existence for me. So people might think: Here we've got another of the usual fools who meet some spirited woman who's inexplicably set on falling in love, and that's what they do, he goes and falls in love with her; and of course she's beautiful, or rich, or titled, or cultured, but what about him? He's just some clod, and a lump and a stumblebum, somebody who works in an office, the kind of lout who ought to have a family, if ever some woman had wanted him, but no woman has, no woman has ever decided to make him the father of her children. So what can you expect? One day the woman walks out. She changes her mind, she takes some whim to somebody else, she's tired of being bored by her fool's conversation, maybe she'll manage at most to break down and cry for a couple of days, and then she's upped and gone. And him? He just sits there and whimpers; he was always boring, and now it's worse; he has this story and he tells it to everybody, and it's such an obvious story and nobody's interested and he tells it so badly and it's all so sad and glum. But he's not about to forget her, since that's just the kind of man he is; instead, he muddles his mind in his fantasies, and once he was only odd but now he's courting madness, an eccentric, and vile, and worthless, and miserable. He's just somebody to be sorry for, but who can be sorry for an abandoned lover who really deserved nothing else? Sure, these are perfectly thinkable thoughts, and why not? It's just that it isn't true, not in the least. First of all, this woman is something that happened by now a long time back, and if I were nurturing an unconcluded love for a woman who disappeared from my life so many years ago, I would now be ripe for an institution. And even, moreover, if I have recognized, and still can recognize, that I am "tied" to this woman, the fact yet remains that I would never really say that I am in love with her, or in any other way a slave to some form of love. But still I say that I am "tied." Certainly this is strange, but not incomprehensible. Take the case of a man who has never had an easy hand with women, nor found it easy to talk with them: a man who, basically, has never succeeded in giving much importance to a woman; and who is convinced, even more basically, that he deserves no more from a woman than sporadic and episodic attention, and that he has never desired otherwise. So, I've had this adventure, and surely some slight experience of love as well, and then everything went back to usual. But now there's a difference, and a large difference: the difference, precisely, that this woman happened; and for her then to have left me doesn't actually count for very much. Once things have happened, they have happened. In a certain way, that woman has never departed this house, which is my house; events exist that remain unchanging among the shifting of moons and suns; not that they are in themselves of enormous importance, but they constitute a different order of events: events which could never have been predicted but that nonetheless took place, and irremediably. If a madman suddenly voices a perfectly cogent, pertinent and illuminating phrase, would we pretend that he didn't say it, simply because it doesn't mesh with the rest of his disheveled discourse? It was impossible for him to speak that phrase, and yet he did. It cannot be canceled out, and nothing ever again will be as it would have been if he hadn't said it. And not simply there in the clinic cubicle, but everywhere, throughout the city, throughout the world, and even throughout other worlds as well, something will have happened that could not have happened: not a miracle, but simply an error. Let's say that I have lived an error. And in doing so I have changed myself, and the people I know, and the city where I live, and perhaps the whole world; since what has happened could not have happened; and what in fact happened, happened in precisely so absurd a way in order clearly to reveal that it was all a question of an error. And how, surely, could I disclaim an error now? What's easy to forget are the things that are right and proper and obedient to socially obvious rules. A marriage engagement, for example. But an error is something else. And here I'd complicate my discourse with a slightly further twist; but if I haven't seemed addled already, the same will hold for the rest. If I say I am "tied" to this woman, it is not impossible that this woman is "tied" to me. Let's get it perfectly straight, moreover, that I don't imagine her ever one day returning to me, maybe with some phrase like: I have never stopped loving you. It's not only that I don't believe it possible, but that I absolutely don't want it. It's clear that the whole dimension of error would be destroyed by a thing like that. Things like that are simply not done, and if it happened it would make for disaster. But this in no way changes the fact that that woman was an essential part of the error; and whether she knows it or not, or knew it or not, error was the center and meaning of what happened to her, just as it was of what happened to me. I ask myself if this woman knows, and how she knows, that she is "tied" to me. Certainly it is possible, and probable, that every now and then I cross her mind, just as all the bits and pieces of a life will chance back into our thoughts because we speak or hear some word. But this isn't what I meant. I ask myself if this woman knows herself to be tied to an event so important as error. Oh, there's no mistaking that she's tied, but does she, I wonder, know it? You can say, of course, she may have repressed everything that happened from her mind. But that doesn't matter. So much the worse for her if she has. I am asking something different. I ask whether she is conscious, aware, and clear within herself of having lived this privilege: the privilege of having lived an error, something without a place in her life and yet undeniably, irremovably there. If that woman is aware of the error, everything else then follows of its own accord; I can even say it's of no importance that she remember me. People will remark: Well that's okay for you, since you've never gotten involved with any other woman, but what do you know about her? Maybe she has a husband, maybe she has been in love with who knows how many men, has had who knows how many affairs. I reply: That doesn't count. In relation to error, the two of us are identical. If I say that I am "tied" to her, it is not because no other image of a woman has taken her place—her place, as they say, "in my heart." I too, in fact, have had a couple of stupid affairs. But I do not want to lose my hold on this stunning center of error, this chosen place within my life that makes the whole and total of my life entirely different from anything else it could have been. We are always surrounded by dramatic events, which in any case take place, but nothing prevents them from being consistent, even in spite of being terrible: a death, a felony, an affront. But this was everything: an affront as well as love. And I repeat that what I intend to describe has nothing to do with feelings; and even less with any lament that I want to submit to the pities of outside ears. I no longer love that woman, and haven't for quite some time; and perhaps I never really loved her; it seems in fact quite probable that there was never any love between us, and this would count as still another signal of error. So maybe it was an infatuation? Never, and not at all: infatuations are not erroneous. I will put it like this: that we encountered an anamorphosis. Or even that certain privileged points exist in which the universe reflects itself deformed, as though its astrological or theological center were flanked by another: a small, round mirror, quite perfectly round and calculatedly convex; and as though the whole of the universe reflected itself within that mirror and took cognizance, not without stupor but free from ire, of an image of itself that it did not know. Error is to find oneself within the curve of that deformed and deforming glass. But it is also a prodigy. And in lives, no matter what they are, so void of prodigiousness, so incapable of prodigiousness, no one ought to repudiate the conservation within himself of a specific "tie": a tie with the absurd and impossibly cogent; something, again, like those impeccable, enlightening words suddenly spoken from a mind obscured in perennial dementia.

What ties me to that man is the undeniable and consoling fact that no other woman would tolerate living with a creature so radically despicable, vile, and morally inert. He is a man one would find it natural to expel from one's life simply not to dirty it with useless and intolerable images. Yet if one were to deduce that I consider myself tied to this man because no other woman would seduce him away from me, or to interpret the word "consoling" as a sign of a difficult, harsh, but not incomprehensible peace, that would be utterly an error. First of all, there are any number of women who love to fall in love with the lowest sort of men, even if then they lack the daring to confront the extraordinary experience that comes in its wake; and I use the word "consoling" in perfect irony, since no relationship could be more wearing, even if there are ways in which I judge it, unsarcastically, to be a good relationship. Perhaps excellent. The essential point, which till now I have left unbroached, is that he knows himself to be despicable, vile, and of no account. And partly that arouses his anger, partly his self-satisfaction. He is an abject creature, but also a creature to whom abjection is natural, and therefore he loves it. There is no way he could be different, and it is therefore right, and absolutely right, for him to be an abject creature. His life gives off a kind of pasty filth that penetrates into the lives of those who know him, and this is an important experience. There is no need to explain how his abjection expresses itself; he is not a delinquent, he is not a criminal. He might be an impostor, but he hasn't the courage to dissemble systematically. His mendacity is constant, but with fibs so badly thought out as never to connect. There would even be no point in telling him he's a liar. As vile creatures are, he is not without gentleness; and since he is abject, he is not without a random intensity, of which he is wholly unaware. And these, as I see it, are the qualities on which our intercourse finds its footing, our "tie." Some people experience intensity in guises of nobility, cultivation, astuteness, dignity, and even of fury; all of that is denied to me. But the flaccid intensity of abjection is utterly familiar, and even if I do not judge myself to be abject, I believe I have a natural capacity for the understanding of everything abject. I will put it better: I believe an intelligence of the abject to give me a route to the center of that intensity from which in other ways I find myself closed off. I am bound to this man by a mixture of impurities, and my reference is not to sexual impurity, but to impurity in modes of handling life, as when a jester's cunning is pressed into service with the gods. He knows that he is abject, but he is utterly unaware of the fundamental meaning of being abject, of what it means in the absolute. He does not know that, and has never known it. So he is necessarily ignorant of why I am tied to him, and I believe him in the depths of his heart, the depths of that miserable heart he has, to be surprised by it, and rather greatly. I've referred to his heart as "miserable." And I see that "miserable heart" could imply a heart continually in need of misericord and compassion, since such mercy in fact is what one grants to a heart reefed by misery. But this, in all sincerity, has nothing at all to do with the feelings I am trying to express. I have no compassion or "mercy" for this man, and I would be very much ashamed of myself if I did. An abject creature isn't to be consoled with abjection. What I feel contains equal parts of scorn and gratitude. And when I use the word "scorn" I ought to add, perhaps a little foolishly, that this scorn is in its own way positive, though I don't know why I add "in its own way." There exists a kind of scorn that doesn't spurn, reject, judge, educate, clarify, illuminate, distinguish or deplore, and that takes no pride in itself. A meticulous scorn for the little things that don't know how or do not want to grow; for the moribund who do not want to die; for the spiritually deformed who lack the daring to do away with themselves. And now as I say these words, I truly understand what I feel. I am tied to this man because he is hostile to growth, indolent in his dying, too great a coward for suicide. All of these "no's" form a system around a pit of darkness, where abjection has its lair. I scorn and despise his verminous will to remain alive, and yet that feculence seduces me. I ask myself if I am tied to a fetus, which is something monstrous, aphasic, and blind, but alive. And surely there is such a thing as a vile fetus, and abject fetuses, delinquent and malignant fetuses, fetus assassins, suicidal, lethal, and fecal fetuses; but all of them show an industry in the custody of their liquid flesh, an industry at continuing to live, and at living in the dark. This man lives in the dark, and I find an exhilaration in how he appears to carry his darkness about with him, as though he were a silhouette of nighttime cut out in the day. He is always dark, no matter the quantity of light, and no matter what kind, that washes over him. This is the way I think I understand the sense in which our tie can nourish itself on a positive scorn. And it's from this that my gratitude is born. Naturally enough, he would find nothing more incomprehensible than what I have called "gratitude." I cull this sentiment and offer it as a tribute to his utter paltriness in his perfect awareness and acceptance of his paltriness, implicitly paying homage to the logical perfection of a project he attempts to oppose with no resistance at all. Even though he does not understand himself, he does nothing to improve himself, and this is something I appreciate, surely, as very few others would dare to do. I owe him my gratitude because his cowardice gives me the image, in reverse, of that center to which my nature aspires in vain. No, he is not a hellish creature; he is a little cramped being that has never unraveled itself from the natural night in which all of us find our sustenance, but that we mix with fragments of dawn and sunset. Living in his company, I have understood abjection; and I have understood that abjection forms a part, and no secondary part, of any tie at all.

What ties me to that woman is the fact that she is ignorant of everything about me and my cruel and vicious life. I patiently worked for years, from the very beginning, to keep her ignorant of everything about me while allowing her still to know those essential things that permitted her, in turn, to be tied to me. I am one of the damned, and have always been, but I feel no desire to spread the contagion to those who are not. A damned man tied to some other undamned creature whom he wants to be tied to him. When I dawdle in a life of calculated monotony with this woman to whom I am tied, she has no way of knowing the complicated rite I execute, no way of knowing my attempt to turn her presence into a kind of guarantee, a useless and fatal guarantee, against myself first of all. No, I do not condemn myself. The careful plot of events, the motions of a naturally unnatural soul, the discomforts of an existence both offended and happy to offend, have worked to prepare me a destiny that it is not up to me to call into doubt, much less to reject. But that very same destiny, fractured and honeycombed like a pomegranate—such an absurd comparison—includes this leathery need for "justification"; and one of its demands, on the pretext of the very condition of my life, the condition that I myself and I alone am to know and practice, is for me to have constructed a condition where I am "tied" to someone and where someone is "tied" to me. Yet all the same it remains quite clearly impossible for her to be "tied" to me, since if she were she would thus participate in my malignant nature, and thereby, this more than anything else, stand implicated, sharing damnation as my accomplice. And the possibility would surely exist for such damnation to find its enactment in her role as witness. But what I want to say is that somehow or another this mutual tie implies, though I wouldn't know how, my awareness that my wretchedness forms a part of it. And since she has no connection with my wretchedness—not because she is innocent, but out of extraneity and indifference—she cannot be my accomplice: she cannot flee in my company across some desert transpierced by the thunderbolts of the minister of destiny. Still, she might stand at the end of that road, with the calm of a slow, smooth body. I can see her there, seated beneath a great tree, with that face of hers as I have always known and perused it, almost expressionless, wise, and pronounced in its structure. In that situation, an entirely imaginary situation, this woman could be a witness: but whether to prove my innocence or my guilt I do not know. Nothing could be less relevant. In terms of our being "tied," what counts is that nothing could be different, and nothing the same, after the delivery of her testimony. No matter whether my iniquity be cited in a catalog of minute and careless but still wholly unpardonable infractions, insults of the soul, and treasonably plotted passions; no matter whether there be a plea in remembrance of the ways in which I gave coherence, through the agency of the "tie," to an otherwise obscure and unnaturally labyrinthine meander, the meaning of which was in any case different from what the woman "tied" to me might have supposed. I have no idea if this delicacy so distractedly poised on the coarse, scaly skin of malignity could be enough to alter a destiny; but my aspiration, rather than to alter, is to confirm a destiny, and the whole of that destiny, including this "tie" that binds us. And it is a matter of utter indifference to me for this tie to act towards effecting my conclusive destruction, or, quite to the contrary, my salvation, since what I demand, in order not to shatter the destiny accorded me—and not without a mysterious pity—is precisely for the tie to act, and to act as such.

As I offer this laborious though somehow forthright description, it will not escape notice that its center is clandestine: there is no question here, in fact, of a tie, but more properly of two ties that encounter one another not directly, but only symbolically, and precisely by virtue of sharing the quality of constituting this unfathomable condition called a "tie." My tie includes the use I make of it against myself, and the awareness as well of its coalescence with a distortion it likewise conceals, which is my name, and that very name with which I was baptized. My distortion thus nurtures and explains the tie, while I myself am yet a part of the distortion, since it in turn is the tie's most deep and cunning gloss. But this woman, on the other hand, is tied to me while ignorant of what constitutes my being tied to her; so her mode of being tied is founded upon another; and perhaps upon the quite precise awareness of "not knowing" who it is that I can be, the awareness of my being but a shadow endowed with a body. This, it strikes me, must be precisely the nature of the tie that she practices: the obscure awareness of being caught up, no matter how vaguely, by what I would call the force, the toughness that a shadow can exercise, in a destiny turned upside down and to be read from no other beginning than shadow itself. So it may possibly be that her tie finds a suffering or enjoyment in this ambivalent presence, in any case drawing a barely conscious color from it. But that tie, finally, can have no choice than to rank as intrinsically different. She is unaware of being called upon to live it as an accomplice or a witness, or that she in fact has been entrusted with a double form of witness, each an alternative to the other while yet perhaps contemporary. Still, I might be in error; indeed, I am certainly in error. She is tied, but her tie cannot be founded on the way I demand a tie; so it will be part of a story, to me unknown, of herself as the subject of a tie. And this then is all that can happen: for me to be unaware of the meaning and configuration of her tie, just as she is unaware of the meaning and configuration of mine. So each of our ties is unknown to the other, and each unaware of the other: and thus, by virtue of that pity I seem to descry in my own unlovable destiny, our ties, in their ignorance, tie together.

II

What ties me to that woman is her refusal: which is not a clear and total refusal, but a cautious, considered, prudent, even discontinuous and sometimes sporadic refusal; just as one speaks of ambiguous relationships, one should also speak of ambiguous distancings. But the refusal that I suffer, and savor, is all the more tying since it grounds itself, if I have understood clearly, on an indispensable presence that I myself must live out surreptitiously within her life. Put it like this: I am indispensable, but precisely as such unacceptable; and so her mode of not accepting me is based on an acceptance far more irreparable than any assenting "yes." I am included in her life, but in a space that is not vital; and this placates my lust to be geometrical.

What ties me to that man is his not unfounded but senseless conviction that for me his presence is indispensable; I should say, however, that in fact he is indispensable, but not really to me as I daily experience myself; he is indispensable to an hypothesis I have always more calculatedly neglected than rejected; since I have never said "no" to this project I have crafted for myself, I am host within the atrium of my soul to a presence that is indispensable only to my hypothesis, which itself, in turn, is both indispensable and constantly denied. My duplicity creates an indispensable place for this man, but determines as well that I, in my entirety, am inaccessible; and I recognize the sophisticated torture of such a situation to be extremely attractive for a man who draws from my duplicity the dark delight of being both accepted and spurned.

What ties me to that woman is her duplicity, her cautious, perspicacious proprietorship of her life while holding on to some kind of fictitious and necessary image endowing her with a form that both fascinates and torments; I know perfectly well that I have no relationship, unless accidental, with that face she administers with so much competence, even if with just as great a portion of reticence, as I see it. But I know that her forms of indulgence in hypothesis, deprived of which she'd find it difficult if not impossible to live, make for a place to which I have access; my rejection is solely due to how this locus of hypothesis holds room for nothing different from rejection. The hypothesis would otherwise cease to maintain its definition.

What ties me to this man is his cognizance, no matter how belabored and reluctant, of my duplicity; since he bears the guilt for it, he, in addition to myself, is the true custodian of my hypothesis; but he has yet another mark, which I can only call pathetic: he has a vocation for rejecting the essence of the hypothesis, meaning the fact that it can only ground itself upon a refusal. But since my refusal strikes no roots into the measurable and solid world of daily existence, it is not a rejection. The "no" he perceives is a "no" not so much connatural with any choice of mine, but with the hypothesis which I, as I must recognize, might perhaps be unable to sustain on my own, even though a "yes" could achieve nothing else than to leave him mortally wounded.

What ties me to this woman is her awareness that what exists between us is not only a relationship, but indeed a tie, and that it rests on the necessity of offering custody to the ambiguous vitality of an hypothesis: and for this tie to find its substance in a "no" rather than a "yes" seems even irrelevant. So my indispensable function is strictly connected to my function as the receiver of this "no." But this too requires clarification: I am myself endowed with the quality of being hypothetical, but with the codicil, through a reversal of terms, that my hypotheticality is identical with my absence; and everything necessary and quotidian about me, or that bears a face and exists in time, is altogether irrelevant, doing nothing to offer me any explanation of myself; I am not a wheel; I am a circle drawn in a space deprived of air. So nothing of what I recite or execute could be executed or recited by others. It would be difficult, moreover, for me to find a woman endowed with any more vibrant sense of the hypothetical, a woman capable of not existing—and thus of rejecting me—with an energy in no way inferior to the energy with which she exists: an activity on which my information is solely second-hand.

What ties me to this man is his intimately geometrical nature, what I would term the "mental" destiny of his figure, at once intolerable and unsubstitutable; I know that only a mental or geometric being could have access to the spaces of hypothesis, which are the ground not yet of the description but of the definition of my destiny, and of all its duplicity. In that sense I can hold him to be indispensable, but I can know such a thing only in the moment I exit from the confines of uncertainty and risk a certain possibility of not being, that state of not being which is my whole temptation, but always on condition that the terms of its celebration be nothing other than temptation. I also know that my hypotheticality furnishes the mental destiny of this man with its only possible space of survival; and therefore that I am indispensable to him.

What ties me to this woman is a contradictory quality: I know her commitment to hypothesis to be a commitment no less my own, in the most rigorous possible way; and it follows that I experience a happiness in having found access to a perigrination reserving no place for anything other than a similarly hypothetical fate; and since this quality is my definition, not my description, so much the more. Yet there is something else that ties me to this woman: and that is her uselessness, which is my own "no." But I want to be utterly clear: the uselessness to which I allude is the luxury, the magnificence, the ornament of life. Now, everything I think is machine-like and spare, uncommonly graceless and unbeautiful; and more than anything else, nothing I think comes to me directly from this relationship; but everything I think most probably stems from it indirectly, which is to say: by traversing the "no." But the "no" in no way ornaments my choices, and what I think bears the night-dark sign of this refusal, the sign both of freedom and solitude. If in a moment of day-to-day liveliness she were to accede to a "yes," which on more occasions than one seemed imminent, if only because her inward awareness of the duplicity in her hypothesis is in fact quite dull, I would have received no benefit from her company. Whereas when restored to her binary nature, she belongs to my life—unaware of it, most probably—precisely due to what "is not there" within her, in no way pertaining to her description, while yet enjoying the obscure privileges of a mental existence, pertaining to her definition.

What ties me to this man is his not ignoble conviction that I represent a luxurious though useless presence. In reality, I have also been created as enigma; and by virtue of what "is not," though nonetheless endowed with incongruous existence, I act upon and constantly interrogate him. And what he believes himself to think—making no mistake, moreover, in defining it as graceless (and could there be any such thing, after all, as a graceful reply to enigma?)—is born from my cryptic nature's distractingness, from out of that interrogation of which I myself am aware of nothing more than the sound.

What ties me to this woman is the exquisite fragility of her hypothetical soul, and even its inexactitude. I have said that I dispose, essentially, of a mental destiny, which I might also define as enigmatic. The singular space of this woman, the thing about her that excites my fascination, is her imprecise reply to a cryptic question, the bloodless pulsation with which a space both of fear and of freedom arises within her—a winged flight, and a game that skirts perilously close to the ecolalia of dementia. A dementia she has in common with me. This delight and this delirium are purely the reply to what something other than myself proposes to her; but I am attired in the enigma and carry it on my body: enigma, perdition, incomprehensible and perhaps impossible salvation.

Travel Notes

I sit within the roofed wooden porch, at my back a minuscule vacant house, and in front of me lies the onset of the candid path of the road. My chair is rustic, not conspicuously comfortable, but not hostile. Before long it will likely begin to rain, and that moment is important, because for as long as it rains the house will be mine. Prevention from going out is not the whole of it, for a change, as I have learned, will also take place in how the house holds its ground; the house will acquiesce to exist as this absurd and pathetic thing: my house. I have no idea of by what amount of space I am separated from the next house, or from the village, given that there is no lack of villages with numerous houses and piazzas, even with hitching rings for horses and troughs for donkeys. This place has been just that attentively crafted. In the distance one likewise catches the glimmer of abandoned parking meters, and spies out a bus station, and I believe heliports as well. Judging from past experience, proceeding from this house to the next should take two to three hours of moderate walking, with calm up-hill stretches and benevolent descents. After every quarter hour, one comes to a bench, always on what to me is the right-hand side of the road, just as all the houses are on the left. Every five hundred yards stands a sideless shed roof, which should it rain is comfortable shelter, even though unprovided with benches or chairs. If rain persists there is nothing to do but crouch down snugly, summon a state of stupor, and refrain from showing the rain any insolence. Great preoccupation with rain is everywhere evident in the region, but not, I imagine, for any purpose of defense. I presume the rain to be a kind of moral clock; its appearances are impediments, but not hostile, and their task is to furnish the road with cadence and interval. As I had foreseen, the rain has begun: incredibly fine and tenuous, no more than a minute rustle. The road rises slowly but at length after the house where I am stopping, and I imagine this singular sound to have been muffled through quiet mountain air. Hard, harsh mountains certainly stand erect behind the fog that rises from the valley, and I think I have made them out, even if the shapes I see might be clouds of a different color. If indeed they are mountains, I will never be able to cross them; my task, when it is not raining, is to walk this road, nothing else. After ten minutes of rainfall I decide to know that the house is mine. I settle into the creaking, rustic chair and let my hands hang down to the sides of my knees. For as long as the rain will last, I have reached my destination. Of course I have no way of knowing how long it will last, but this tiny drizzle might continue into the night, perhaps until dawn. If I have reached a destination, I can unpack my bags. And since of course I have no bags, I unpack them mentally and distribute the underwear, the change of suit, and the pair of neckties into the various closets the house provides. I will ask my wife to put my shirts away in the chest of drawers and to iron my jacket. Obviously my wife does not exist, but for as long as it rains I am not required to remember that. If I listen with intense, absent-minded attentiveness, I hear noises at my back and certainly they are creakings of wood and of half-open windows touched by wind. Yet nothing prevents me from considering these noises to be indications of my wife, and I know her to be busy and obedient even in addition to extant. Every time the rain has induced me to make a stop, I have caught these very same noises; but no others. So I have to admit that my wife, who is probably a different wife at every station, is always silent, and her silence always total. I do not know if she has nothing to say, as so often happens with long-married couples, or whether cultivating the softness of that silence is a privilege very dear to her, so that I as well as she can cuddle up within it to our comfort. Now that the rain is a little more intense, giving guarantee of a few hours span of tranquil possession of this way-station house, I can also allow myself at least one son. But I think that, no, I will choose a daughter. I am a man of very few words, and I have no desire for a restless son—how would I reply to his questions?—and a daughter might be of some company to my taciturn spouse. It would be still more reasonable to choose a person advanced in years, if not for my fear of their cautionless tongues. If the father of my wife were with us, I would be quite ill at ease, since it might be discourteous to smoke a pipe or raise my voice on account of some deafness. In reality, no one during these stop-overs has ever addressed a word to me, I have never seen anyone, and this, if it does not make me happy, fills me with placid contentment, like a person playing with pebbles. What takes place, in short, is a change in the quality of the noises: if it were not raining, I would know their causes; but it rains, and the noises outline faces and bodies and people and a bustling domestic life devotedly conducted by persons with a loving interest in my felicity. If there were a nearby newsstand, I could send my son or my daughter to get a paper; but here, of course, there are no such things as newspapers, and I have one less reason for setting these fragile noises to a test. The evening is descending, hastened by the constant hushing of the rain; great banks of fog gleam with whitish lights over beyond the road, and I lower my eyelids as I think it will soon be time for dinner.

The meal will be light but pleasant, and tomorrow, the rain having finished, I will have to resume my walking. No one hurries me, and I like to walk slowly. When I rise and make my way to the room where meals are taken, I find the table laid, the chairs drawn up around it. From the number of the chairs, and the type, I can sometimes decipher the composition of my rainy-day family. Here the chairs inform me of a wife, a son, and someone else whom I can't make out: perhaps a grandfather, an aunt, or a visiting friend, hopefully not a physician for a wife who is frequently out of sorts. This extra chair is no rarity, and even though it left me slightly troubled me on the first few occasions, I limit myself now to thinking it an allegorical presence, or a mere allusion. It might very well be, after all, that our family is hospitable. Dinner is ready. In fact it is always ready. On my entering the main room of every house in which I have ever stopped, dinner has every time been ready, and the chairs, variously arranged, around the table. I eat the agreeable food, a few cooked greens and a soft, viscous cheese, and I drink an excellent wine. I am content to spend a rainy evening in the midst of people who are dear to me, and if I look at the chair set off to one side I know I am host to an affable guest who can talk of his travels and experiences in a rich and colorful way while never giving offense to a lady. The evening darkens, and were it not for the warmth of these human presences, I might feel alone.

Being master in this house, I can quaff a small last glass of good wine and then rise to my feet to wish a good night to my family and guest, the nod of my head both absent-minded and affectionate. I take a few turns beneath the protecting porch roof while the rain beyond falls dense and uniform. I am not certain that my guest has not followed me—his discretion is impeccable—and if I have taken a seat, I imagine him in turn to sit behind me, since I catch not so much as a glimpse of him, even from the corner of my eye. A pendulum clock from within the house strikes an hour, which can be any hour at all, but always and clearly alluding to sleep. I am grateful for the house, the placid family, the guest, the food, the rain. This brief repose will contain no harm. I cross back through the house and retire to my room. With a calm voice I say good-night, and am greeted by a low, chorused rush of water, wind, creaking wood and clock-ticks sufficient even for a numerous family, or for a populous reunion of friends.

The bed is soft, wide, and fresh. I know I will sleep in it for only a single night, which is why I regard it with affection and want it to know that I do not intend to forget it; I consign it my form for the whole of a night, throughout which length I shall have been wholly defenseless. Surely, if I so desired, I might even prolong my stay through two nights; strictly considered, I might even ignore the possible disappearance of the rain and remain in this friendly bed. I know I would find a ready lunch and dinner, but I would find no wife, no son, no guest. I sleep soundly, even if the infant's surrender to sleep is something I haven't experienced for years. I dream frequently: dreams concerned with the road I walk, the houses, the family. Still, they are strangely unpeopled dreams, and even if I nurture the habit of glossing them, it does not strike me that I see them as holding anything more than circumstantialities of meanings, and of meanings in any case vile, or unnecessary. At any rate, they are dreams unencumbered with anguish. In these dreams I am strangely small, even minuscule, even though I could not indicate the unit of measure by which I judge myself. I don't intend to say that this is the case in all of my dreams, but when I am large, my stature is gigantic; so I should imagine the unit of measure, in all probability, to be myself, which results in inability to see myself. On some rare nights, I am visited by dreams that are blandly prophetic: I glimpse the shape of the house I will visit a few days hence; as I listen a week or so later to the noises that constitute my wife, I will recognize a rhythm that I dreamed during a night of rain.

I love this nocturnal silence, and would like to say so to someone. I sometimes deplore my habit of sleeping alone. But if, on the other hand, I were not alone, how could I comment on the silence except by marring it? I recognize my solitude to contain a certain amount of wisdom.

I awaken, it is still night. I sharpen my ear and understand what is taking place. There is no doubt; the guest has gone. Whoever he may be, he alone can walk with impunity in the rain, so long as it is fine and clement. My son—or my daughter—is a flimsy nothing, and my wife disintegrates. If I deciphered the noises with a crueler attention, I would recognize that all that remains of my wife is a shock of hair, an eye, a little heap of fingers. The rain is drawing to a close. The bed-sheets are distracted and inattentive. The pendulum intolerably slow. I think it is time to ready my bags, though probably my wife will have done that, probable too that no one will have touched them, everyone being aware of the ephemeral while solemn character of my sojourn; and finally I believe to have grasped the knowledge that there are no bags, nor ever will be. So I shall not pick at myself about the dawn, which already I recount to myself as cold and grey, the large rocks lucent with rain, the irritated and ungraspable odor of the wakeful grass with no more dreams. I allow myself a further lapse into a dreamless, brief sleep. I know that during these seemingly unpeopled dreams I busily work within myself at not proving unworthy of the further unfolding of the road; yet still I have the impression that I over-evaluate my duties. With no hostility in my smile, I tell myself that I am the head of my family.

When I get out of bed, I have neither wife nor children; I discover no patterns in the noises and take no interest in them. I hurry about, but am in no hurry. I have asked myself whether "my family" remains in that house, awaiting another voyager, another myself. Yet they are not an integral part of the house, because if they were they would not cease to be there as soon as my moment for departure grows imminent. Certainly they are a part of the stop-over, but I am unconcerned with knowing in precisely what way. I eat standing up, I want the house to understand, and addressing no farewell to anyone I return to my walking.

On my left, the road is delimited by a continuous border of rocks, and by more attractive stretches of mountains; on the right I see a declivity, which I presume concludes in a valley. The sky is crisscrossed by great clouds, and the light, never revealing its source, which most certainly is hidden by what I continue to presume to be an impervious chain of mountains, dissolves into the air and reaches me cold and grey. Yet if I felt inclined to a contemplative view of my itinerary, I would have to avow that the place, though severe, is amenable; and I might linger in descriptions of the varying colors of green, and the scaly rocks, and the flimsy tissue of the banks of fog. But I am conducted in my progress, slow as it is, not I would say by impatience, but by attention; I examine the things I encounter, whether rock or grass, as though I ought to recognize them, or in any case should hold them in mind. I come to the first bench, on my right; it is still wet with rain and dawn. I set one foot before the other, and every now and then I cast a glance towards the sides of the road; every now and then—I couldn't say how long—I stop and swivel quickly about on my feet to look behind me. The house I left has ceased already to be visible; but this stretch of the road bends continuously to the left. I count the trees that rise at intervals along its edge, bizarrely giving it the air of an avenue, a place to stroll with little children or to march along classes of school boys. Before setting out again I look all around me, to the front and all sides; when walking I keep my gaze trained steadily on the short stretch of road directly before me, whereas now I allow myself to look as far ahead as I can. I see the road unravel, and then it slips from view. It reappears much further ahead—at perhaps two or three days of walking—and a singular emotion arises as I see that I am not to reach a house, no matter how large, but something with the aspect of a castle or a village. That places such as these exist along the road is something one learns quite early on; at the very beginning of the road one leaves behind a kind of derelict hamlet where someone apparently spent whole centuries, some of them still future centuries, uninterruptedly constructing, even if there is no telling for whom, if not for inhabitants who all died or emigrated. The curious thing about villages is having access to a variety of houses, if they are not boarded up, and in sensing their several proposals of families and friends.

Even when a village seems to have been left unpeopled for centuries, or forever, it is not rare to find a lingering odor of horses, and of dogs. And so great a number of doors and windows and thresholds and chimney pots makes for the hearing of unthinkable noises, and one imagines oneself molested by a thronging crowd. Sleeping in villages means dreaming agitated dreams, sometimes reawakening long before dawn and finding no repose. After that first one, I saw another village, though considerably at a distance, perched on the flank of the mountain; I do not know if some other road leads up to it, different from the one I am walking; I formulate questions, not without amazement and even fear. I ask myself whether in that one there are persons who resemble me, or if it stands deserted like the one encountered at the start. Of another that I reached and left behind me in the night—for it is not forbidden to proceed by night, even if one quickly learns to lose whatever enthusiasm for doing so—I remember no more than the looming blackness of a small clump of houses I assumed to be closed, even though I left their doors untried.

I return to walking. The light has grown harder, and while losing none of its coldness has taken on a noonish quality. I have already said that I proceed without haste, though never with negligence. In reality I am very calm. I am not happy, nor would I claim a right to be; I do not, as must be clear, make plans, but I feel a hard calmness solidly wedged inside me, with its center in my belly. I think that what I meant to say while talking of my attentiveness has now grown clear. Since I am to walk, only and absolutely to walk, I walk with attention. There is a pedantry in my walking, and pedantry is not a virtue that furnishes contentment or a sense of self-fulfillment. Surely I have no reason to be proud of myself, which does not mean, however, in any way at all, that I hold myself in contempt. Such a state of mind, and how it grounds itself on the careful execution of a slow and patient task, favors calm: a calm which I do not pretend shows kinship with, as they say, "a soul at peace with itself," whatever that may be. I imagine a soul at peace with itself to know a condition of light, happy, illuminated spirit, and I have an impression of this "peace" as something restless and noisy. Perhaps I do not like it, or it has nothing to do with me. I greatly prefer my calm—not entirely bare of a touch of dishonesty—since it feeds on my relationship with the road. Just as I have a relationship with every house or bench where I stop or rest, or that I simply see, I likewise have a relationship with the road, which for a great deal of time was an extremely difficult relationship. Even though recalling it is more than arduous and unwelcome, I cannot forget that the road seemed tiring, frustrating, and ironic. I would walk by night and eat standing up, and I ignored the attentions of wives who were certainly deserving of a better husband. I would talk to myself as I walked, and sometimes would stand on the benches to see how long a stretch of road was opening out before me. I would even leave signs behind me as though to make it known, perhaps to the road itself, that I had not abandoned the notion of turning back and retracing my steps. Once I climbed to the roof of a house to look as far into the distance as possible. I would walk in the rain and had the impression of discerning a kind of charity in those tepid tears. I wasted my energy in vague, useless gestures, declaiming improvised verses and scrutinizing the edges of the road in the attempt to make out traces of other passers-by or signs that might help me calculate the distances from one way station to the next. I wept and behaved in ways neither virile nor trustworthy. I left highly intricate messages on tables of houses I was leaving, messages that blended lamentations with a self-satisfaction in proffered collaborations, complicities conceived by a kitchen scullion. I offered to dust the trees and to draw up and set out road signs, if only I might be furnished with the place names. Once I went so far as to pretend to abandon a house, only then to return to it in hopes of finding some reply. That is the only time I have ever retraced my steps along a stretch of the road, walking it three times in all. A moment of horrid desperation. Turning back towards the house was already monstrous, forcing me to look at things in an order in which they were not meant to be looked at, an order running counter to their very way of being: it was an act submerged in anguish, made tolerable only by my extremity of unhappiness. But the third stretch of road, on my second departure from the house, was excruciating, and not tolerable at all. Scrolled for still a third time, those images seemed imbued with a lurid familiarity, fleshy and devastated. I loved and hated every slightest object, and these objects observed me in turn with a calculated impotence that wracked me with pain. While walking, moreover, I knew very well that I had simply lengthened my path by two equal stretches; retracing my steps meant rediscovery of the lacerations of a whole stage of travel I had thought already behind me. Ever since, I have made it a careful habit, whenever I stop and turn around, to take off my shoes and move to a position a step ahead of them. My shoes defend me, and by never stepping past them, I guarantee my avoidance of the error of turning back, even by so much as a single step. What consumes and tortures is the very structure of turning back.

I have not said whether there in that house I found anything that might have been thought a reply. Crossing that threshold was to suffer an atrocity. I found no reply, but simply noted that my scrap of writing had been removed. I do not know if someone had picked it up, or if it had simply been discarded in the act of relieving the house of the many signs of my reckless disorder.

After the experience of tripling a section of the road, I treated its further sections, as I walked them, with taciturn fear. And I consider it an act of providence for a protracted rain to have forced me to stop—for the exceptional length of three full days—in a congenial house among indications of a mild and indulgent family, its members perhaps of subnormal intelligence.

Perhaps I will talk about that stop-over, though I do not see what sense such talk might have; what I now desire is to make it clear that my state of mind from that moment forward went rapidly through a change: from an amicable melancholy to a delicate discretion, to an affectionate and guilty diligence, to a wise and irritating imperturbability, and from there to the final issue of this poor, unadorned calm that shares nothing with desperation and nothing with hope, that makes no calculations, that never is more than barely disturbed or else neatly successful at concealing all sense of disturbance whenever it catches, as now, a glimpse of a distant village.

As I proceed, slowly, toward the next way station, which I do not yet see—the road now winds and twists, and vision is checked by tatters of fog—I find it opportune to give clarity to what otherwise remains implicit in these notes I lay before myself. First of all, my travels along the road take place in total solitude. I have never met another person, nor have I seen any traces of voyagers who might have preceded me. Everything would lead me to believe that this road was constructed for but a single voyager, and that that voyager is me. I find this conclusion to hold no motive either for pride or for dejection. I do not believe that the road is mine or was constructed for me expressly, simply that it was constructed for a single voyager. For me to be that voyager establishes no special relationship with the road, only with the voyage. The road is support for a voyage, and it is I who execute the voyage. It strikes me not as unreasonable to suppose the voyage to be a part of the road, or is the voyage perhaps the road in a state of motion? In any case, I do not possess the road; I am a property of the voyage, which in turn is a property of the road.

This solitude, then, neither alarms nor frustrates; and it is hardly precise to call it solitude, since by walking I lend the road a justification. Yet this function demands stability and lucidity; it requires calm. My calm is a part of how the road functions. This is why it cannot abandon me, nor escape my control. If I entertained the admission—entertaining absurdity—that some other walker were approaching me, or following rapidly on my heels, my calm would be impossible. If another voyage were to intertwine with mine, I would have to defend myself through every possible means, and ferociously. My voyage coincides with the road, and I demand the totality of the road, and the totality of the voyage. My solitude and slowness coincide with my calm. Nothing spurs me on, calls me, waits for me, or follows me. I might think of the road as a long low building, and of myself as wending through it, indifferently and attentively.

When I speak of solitude, perhaps I ought to add that not only have I never encountered persons, but not even animals. If I turn to examine the valley I see nothing that might seem a sheep, or a goat, or a cow, even though the territory is rich with grass and water and would reasonably exert an attraction on shepherds with their herds. I have never caught the indistinct flight of a bird in the sky. I have never heard a chirping in the grass, or a song, a trill or a cooing from the greenery of a tree. I have never sighted flowers, and the only odor is the hard, watery smell of grass. I ask myself, I do not know how idly, what might happen if ever I should meet an animal: a cat, I think, or a toad at the edge of the road. I think I would have to consider them as forming a part of the voyage I perform. Still they would modify the voyage, though proposing no different voyage. I ask myself if the voyage might fall ill, and I am certain I make no mistake in replying that the voyage will not fall ill on condition that I preserve my calm, even if it find itself confronted with the villainous presence of a beast, or an insect.

When I speak of solitude, I refer, of course, to the stretches from one way-station stop to the next, to the voyaging. My condition in way-station places is different. I have asked myself whether I continue to be in voyage while residing in one of these houses, or if the voyage is to be understood to have been suspended. I have concluded that the voyage knows no interruptions. What I define as stop-overs are sections of the itinerary, not in terms of the road, but a traveling nonetheless. First of all, I do in fact move within these way-station houses, executing figures on their floors, which figures are most certainly necessary to the voyage; and when I remain almost immobile, seated or asleep, I execute minimal designs; and even were it thinkable that I achieve an absolute immobility, that immobility would again be a part of the workings of the road. Yet solitude remains a term ill-fitted to my condition in my stop-over houses. I am a figure drawn by the road—and the road is not drawn by me—but the noises, creakings, and rusty whinings of the houses are surely drawings of my own. This is how I have a family, children, and guests. In those hours I live a populous existence. The fact that the persons with whom I sojourn are always elsewhere, in another room, or on the porch when I am in the house, is part of their appointment and, as well, a witness to their affection, which comforts and assists me. I cannot deny that these stop-overs are often cheerful, domestic in the most traditional way, and innocently soothing. I cannot deny my love for the children's ingenious games, the solicitude of a placid spouse, the sober splendor that comes to surround me in the much appreciated company of a friend, a guest. As I said before, I never catch sight of any of these persons I speak of as children, wife, and friend. I speak with none of them. And yet I am with them, and my being while there in those places is replete with the quiet joy that comes from pacific, well-trod conversation. It must also be added that I am greeted at every stop-over by a different family, which yet is always my very own family, and has been since the beginning of time. Described by gusts of wind through half-closed windows, or by the lazy swaying of hinges, there is a succession of cheerful, taciturn, maternal, friendly, affectionately absent-minded or alertly attentive wives: but in every instance I rediscover the abundance of delight with which they greet me, seeing just how great a joy the children find in my arrival, always expected and always unforeseeable, and just how much they all would want to recount if only I didn't invoke the protection of my happy weariness. In reality, I am not fatigued at all. But this pretended weariness confers me some right to expect the indulgence of those who are near to me, and it grants me license to forestall the delightful moment of our confidences, games, re-evocations and hopes. I remain protected by my lassitude until the rain is over; until I decide, my tiredness gone, that it is time to return to my walking. To be thorough, I should make mention too of the principal signal which tells me that the time has come to leave. The noises change and attenuate. I understand that wife and children and friends are disappearing: the whole of a life we might have perfected together! I feel a vague regret, yet tempered by a sense of profound relief; in the moment when the solitude of the road retakes possession of the house, I know I must leave. There are no farewells, just as there were never conversations. Plans are made, but never discussed. There are no caresses. I eat alone, since I am highly respected. When my loved ones crumble apart, I leave a possible life behind me, and I resume my real itinerary. I do not turn around to look at the house, even though I am a naturally affectionate person and, I believe, a decorous father and lovable husband, even if I cannot say to whom.

I realize it might be maintained that my solitude continues even at these way stations. Yet in my knowledge of the solitude of the road, I see it as the recapitulation of every possible solitude, such that every other solitude by comparison takes the guise of a teeming crowd of friendship, of love, or a family. I must add that I exit from these houses exhausted by even such tender contacts, and only after a long stretch of road will I rediscover a foretaste of the volatile pleasure of arriving at home.

An inconsistent splash of rain makes me scrutinize the sky, livid purple and white with low clouds. I see a shed roof and take refuge. I ask myself what meaning these sheds may have in relation to the road and the voyage. They offer something singularly elusive: beneath these roofings I find the solitude of the voyage and the repose of a house. Yet here I have neither wives nor children. In the moment I halt beneath a shed roof, I always find verification that my solitude is active only while I walk. No matter how briefly I stop, I feel that solitude abandon me, even if nothing replaces it. I find myself, with respect to solitude, in a condition of desire, of tenderness, and of love. I feel affection for the solitude that subtracts itself, just like a lover who loses the woman he loves in the midst of a crowd. No sooner than the rain is over, I quickly plunge back to the center of my solitude. A shed roof allows me to comprehend to just what extent my solitude and calm are one and the same: my solitude, I could say, and the voyage, the rain, the road, the calm.

No, I will not quicken my pace. I have been walking now for a while, and the air is humid, but my new home should not be far away. I round a curve, and I see it. Every time I remark the house that is soon to become my own, I stop to examine it. I could reach it in just a few minutes, but prefer to delay. I must always have an interval in which the sensation of arrival can swell up within me. A partial arrival, naturally, but arrival for that very reason. Since I surprise myself at desiring both the arrival and departure, rest and flight all at once, my calm holds itself in balance between these two contrasting states of mind; it hovers but does not disperse. I know I am not to reach the house with the customary stride with which I walk the road; I am to dissemble some kind of impatience, a nostalgic weariness—which will serve, as I have said, to protect me. I will mimic warmth and feel finally that I have warmed. I arrive with trifles of stories and necklaces of memories. But this time, what will my wife be like? Will I finally have a daughter? Will I have a large countrified bed, the sort of bed I most love? When I see myself to have entered the pertinent frame of mind, I again begin to walk. This house seems larger than the last, is dark with mountain timber, has a tall sharp roof and the customary porch, and I already note the rustic chair that will cater to my repose. The house is densely surrounded by shrubbery still dripping with rain. Already I seem to hear a noise, as of someone bounding quickly up the stairs. I do not know if that window thrown wide open, perhaps in the bedroom, is the work of the wind, or of a hand. I come to a halt at the porch; again I have arrived.

With the halting motions, as always, of a man advanced in years, I take my seat on the simple, bare chair that awaits me for a brief, unique encounter in the course of the centuries. As always, once seated, I listen—to decipher the family that has so long awaited me, so soon again no longer to exist. The quality of the creakings is this time unexpected, and the wind courses through the house with a sound of fatigued lamentation. I lower my eyelids and investigate. Little by little I realize that this time there will be no festive greeting, none of the wonder of friendly words around a table. Something terrible has happened during my absence; and I reflect, with the adumbration of a smile, that some such thing could hardly not have happened since my absence dates from always. Now I know: my daughter is dead, the daughter I so much desired, the indulgent companion who lent her ear to my wandering senile loquacity. I have lost the girl I have never known and whose life is an object of my total ignorance, the girl I could not have recognized had we ever chanced to meet. I do not know her age, nor the games she played, nor her flashes of wisdom, nor her profile, nor the sound of her voice. So the loss is absolute. Or I could say, more precisely, that this daughter was projected as loss from the very beginning, and projected by the road itself: as loss, as absence, as dead. I investigate to see if she had brothers. I suspect a brother, therefore a son, but a son reluctant and hostile at seeing his father's arrival. I understand him. I bear no guilt, but am yet to taste the narrow domestic cramp that guilt inflicts upon my home. Why was I so far away while that house, which is my house, was overwhelmed with tragedy? I could respond that I was far away since that is the only place where I can be. My son replies I should have been "here," since "here" is my home. I nod my head in assent, though of course we both are lying; I must be punished, my son must punish me. I could defend myself by affirming that this house is not "here," and is thus no place in which I could have been, just as I cannot be in it now. But I cannot defend myself, nor would I want or know how to defend myself. It is only within that straitened space of a "here"—more narrow than a pin-point—that defense is possible or, better, licit, even if always unadvised. My son's resentment is enormous; his father disappointed him; my stalwart virile presence had failed him and in absence had worked as no stave against his headstrong, youthful pain. By virtue of the single fact of then having been in that "far away" which is the only locus I possibly inhabit, I committed a dereliction of love. I do not defend myself, and I know that this is my crime, the act for which I must be punished. I attempt to display humility, my hands miming motions of reassurance that such things must never again be allowed to happen. I know I will not be forgiven, and I do not ask for forgiveness, surely out of no taciturn pride, but from the conviction of having no right to it. I look for my wife. Not even she had awaited me with an air of hope, or trusted the renewal of my presence to be a harbinger of slower and happier days. Penned up within the walls of a house that does not love me, that reproves and accuses me, my wife makes no attempt to shield my eyes from a face overstamped with anger and mourning. She had placed her love in an unworthy man—a man, no matter whether absent-minded or fatuous, who was unanswering to himself, to her, and to duty. My arrival is to a place that considers me a deserter, a place that judges itself as having been abandoned, by me. In the silence of my walking, I had already known I would come to such houses: houses so private and personal as to offer no haven, no matter how flimsy, no matter how conventional; houses where all I might find would be accusations, lamentations, denunciations, early deaths, abandonments, reluctancies, interrogations, these restless gestures, these unrespecting, offensively commonplace phrases. I can comfort no one; I can find no forgiveness in my son; I cannot ask my wife what has happened during my absence: nothing less than my absence itself has created this house, and my son who is pain, and my daughter who is death, and my wife who is rancor. This house is my not being there; I must recognize that my "far away" is intolerable. By now it is night, I cautiously rise from my chair, I return to my walking. The night is dark, the house at my back shows no light at any window, what would happen if someone were now to call out to me?—which has never happened and cannot happen. Guilt defends me. I walk just barely lighted by the phosphorescence of the low clouds; but the road is intensely white and shimmers with every nighttime light of stars and gibbous moons. This is not the first time I have walked at night, but walking at night will, every time, surprise me. In reality I cannot lose my way, I cannot walk unawares past a shed, a bench, or a house, yet the road by night is in its own turn far away. Pressing forward is arduous, and my calm is sorely put to test. What do I fear if I know, as I do, that I will encounter no one? Perhaps, at night, I actually encounter him: this no one who bears my own features and shares my futile and ruinous existence, but consciously—without love and without error. I am possessed by envy for my shadow, for an empty and desolate profile of myself, worn and intact.

My pace is regular, never hurried, always sure and

attentive; yet my ear hears something nocturnal in the quality of the rhythm of my feet, as though their advance were assisted only by my calm, or my recent punishment, and not by the road's collaboration. Here, however, I speak inexactly, for the road does not collaborate; all the indications that it offers are tautological and repetitive, saying nothing if not that this is the road. I could say that by night the road does not speak of itself at all, but this again is inexact: I prefer to say that by night the road alludes to itself through fragments of dreams from which I myself am excluded, if not as something dreamed that itself is unaware of the dream.

I pass three benches and two sheds; I note a distant sound of water, doubtless a stream at the bottom of the valley. The first dawn light overtakes me just as I have left a vast shed roof, solitary and unstable, behind me. It isn't raining, so it has been no mistake to travel throughout this night. Here now is another house.

This time I will not stop. And I believe that this is the very first time I have chosen not to consider the appearance of a house as a proposal that I think it my own, as a suggested arrival. The decision not to stop is immediate, and without discomfort. There are manifold reasons that induce me not to stop, all mutually inconsistent. I believe my lack of love must be punished, but equally resolve that I do not want punishment from the beings of any "here." After my daughter's death I could not tolerate another little exemplary family where everything is perfect and picturesque; yet the death of my daughter determines as well that the only stop I might find tolerable would lie at the very heart of the picturesque. I have entered a condition where the houses both proffer and exclude themselves for the selfsame reasons, and also for their opposites. I wonder if I will ever again concede myself a stop-over in these houses, or if any such stops would be granted me. I ask myself whether any further houses will dare to accost me as the possible recipient of their tender, ephemeral attentions and likewise ephemeral mournings.

I ask myself what this may mean for the road: whether I am approaching some stage or place or sign that will alter my voyage; something, for example, that will render my calm inadequate. The question is casual and thoroughly absent-minded. I know all questions on the voyage to be utterly superfluous. They can expect no reply, and not even to be considered.

I pass slowly before the house I reject and I look with vague irony at the chair on the porch, as though discovering only now that this chair is always one and the same, always transported to precede my arrival, from one house to another. I make no attempt to understand what family I abandon in that house, and I am certain as I look at the doors and windows that no one will attempt to remind me of duties and acts of devotion for which I forever and irreparably have ranked as too low. Then, before long, a twist in the road, and the house lies hidden. The day begins to assume its form like a fetus somewhat late in choosing to be a person.

I thus defect from the domestic antagonisms of my solid, ephemeral homes, and my innocent profile leaves desolate houses behind it: desolate, or simply forgetful, and intent upon an innocence the features of which I am not to know. I rediscover the slow and measured pace of an always attentive voyager, always passing through, and free, as always, of impatience. The road has grown little by little more narrow, and on my left, where under other conditions my houses might rise, extends a monotonous expanse of grass, saddened by dust that knows only the irritation of the wind. Were I to detect within that grass an indication of a project for a house, I would be forced to suppose, quite without rancor, that someone more worthy than I will someday be destined to travel this same itinerary. But I detect nothing. At the end of the curve that erases all sign of a house, of a wife, and of children, a sharply falling valley reveals itself before me, the enormous, candid boulders at its floor seeming to mingle with the dry, faint outline of a streambed; and at the head of the valley I can now, doubtless, discern the rise of tall, indifferent peaks. I imagine them impervious and dramatically steep—even if from this distance they acquire a resemblance to enormous, smooth, triangular pebbles, softened by quiet mantles of fog. The road, the valley and my steps all move in that direction, but I know those mountains to bear no relation to the landscape with which they seem continuous. Yet it would not be inexact to maintain that an obstinate, tranquil course might one day reach them. Or beyond. I smile.

On my right I see a bench: two pieces of wood, worn and consumed even though never having been put to use by anyone. Is it possible that my slowness and these very memories I believe myself to carry so lightly prove intolerable and corrosive to the objects I encounter? Is it possible that I am a sickness, a nightmare, an anguished conjecture or hypothesis of the road I am walking? And mightn't the looming of these distant mountains be a gesture of menacing terror, almost in reply to my slowly unfolding progress and as though I threatened them with contagion. But I lack any real inclination for fantasies in anomalous presumption, and must therefore suppose that what I think is nothing more than a game of bored imagination. I am not impossibly the boredom of the road, but nothing more.

The large, dark blot that straddles the road comes

distantly into view. I am not surprised. In fact I feel a contained relief, as though for quite some time I had been waiting for that image; indeed, as though something within me had begun to demand it.

I know that what I have sighted is not a house, nor a hotel, nor a temple, even though partaking of all of these callings. As I advance, the image grows larger, and in like time disintegrates. Now I am fairly close. It is a village: a hamlet surrounded by a palisade just slightly taller than a man; beyond its staves can be seen the roofs as well as the upper storeys of many buildings. A gate stands open in the fence; its halves oscillate in the tenuous wind. I enter the village.

Once through the gate, I find myself in a narrow alley, which gives access to a perfectly regular square. I am surrounded by wooden houses, erected on low, stone foundations. My gaze encompasses a question: whatever can these buildings be? I train my ear and hear nothing but the customary, imperfect silence of the valley. Shutters sway back and forth, curtains perhaps tremble. The village is deserted. No house has bolted doors and I dare to look. In this house I see a long, rectangular table, an orderly sequence of chairs; before each chair, on the table, a polished wooden plate. I suppose it to be a tavern. But no, it must be a school and this is its refectory. Something sour and still unripe, the immaturity of an alphabet not yet memorized, remains on the walls. An imposing chair has certainly hosted the teacher: the man who knew. The order of things is precise, like the cleanliness, but not perfect, as could hardly be otherwise in a place that swarms with young and impatient creatures. I return to the square.

I walked at length through the streets of this deserted but not desolate village. Even though I found no sign of life, nor heard a sound, nor could fantasize that just around a corner I would chance upon the antique sleep of an aged dog or the clattering of a child alone at play, everything seemed arranged for a theater of life, or perhaps constructed in expectation of the invention of life. I observed the square embellished by dry fountains; and around these fountains the comfortable benches, invitations to festive or hair-splitting conversation. A deserted saloon offers stools for men with the gift of facile and audacious gab. Playgrounds have been established for precipitous infant games; commodious benches allow mothers and grannies to heed that none of their charges come to grief through the fervor of their own interior existence. This is a village of meditated purpose where the young must marry, infants be born, and parents grow old with no curiosities beyond these fragile confines; and where the cemetery is finally to gather the empty shells—the one then the other—that were once alive and certainly not incapable of love. I might suppose the inhabitants of this hamlet all to be dead, but I know that no epidemic, no war, no folly of internecine destruction, no famine has ever frequented this place. Even if were I to find the cemetery, it would be only a resting place of possibilities, free of all memory of pain. I must therefore believe that all of those who bit by bit will come in time to populate the meekness of this village are somewhere else, in a place to which access is denied me: a place for the orderly storage of the voices, the gestures, the refusals, the assents, the wrathful births, the unassuming deaths. But it may also be that these imaginary villagers are immersed in a solid and ancient sleep from which they contemplate no reawakening. Or it could be that this village has only just now been abandoned by a vociferous piebald crowd somehow or another advised of my imminent arrival; that everything meanwhile has nicely been put into order and endowed with a not illegitimate expectation of life: whether the town is abandoned or has been offered before me on display, almost as an act of surrender, is something I am not to know, just so long as I renounce all sight of its inhabitants, all ambition to talk with them. Have the hamlet dwellers hidden in the grottoes, in the clefts within the valley? Do they hold their breath, and listen for my footsteps, and clasp hands over the mouths of children so they will not cry or laugh? Though I do not believe this, I behave like a guest unjustly judged invasive and a source of harm; yet I am not unaware that the malice of my existence may lie in something other than what might be conjectured as my hostile soul. Slowly I walk the streets and set doors ajar while at the same time cautious to leave no trace that might appear discourteous and ill-considered. My mind shapes hypotheses about the buildings I see. This, perhaps, is the house where the elderly gather, and make their decisions on how best and most minutely to foster the fragile eternity of the village life that surrounds them. And that is a church; entirely in wood, the doors thrown open, the pews aligned. But I see no writings, nor a painting, nor an image on the walls, nothing that tells me the slightest thing at all about the nature of any faith, as though the fugitives had decided to make no revelation of their innermost beliefs; or if they are immersed in their unfathomable sleep, it would be rather as though their future faith had not yet been fully honed, and were waiting for the final hand of an authoritative theologian. I laugh and exit from this church that clearly has no desire for inevitably faithless supplicants, since it offers no signs of any faith that would befit it. I am always and everywhere passing through, but here I have no choice than to pass through in sacrilege.

I will spend the night in any house at all; I know I will find no traces of relatives, no memories of loves. I ascend the steps to an entrance and enter a bare room; on the wall I notice an empty coat rack. A flight of stairs leads to an upper floor. The stairs creak, an ironic fiction of life. At the top of the stairs, a half-open door gives me access to a room; against the wall a minuscule bed. I lie down, and, as though something had awaited that gesture, I feel the night close around me with a light rustle; and as I fall asleep, I believe I hear noises from the square, from the streets, perhaps songs from the church. Perhaps I am the sleep of the villagers, and only my dreams set them free. Where is what we dream when we are awake? I wave a hand, wanting the dimensions of my benevolence to be understood, the extent of my friendship towards these people's existence. I want to make it clear that if every night I go to sleep it is only to hear for a moment, to believe I hear, the tremulous sounds of the life they live. This is the vainest imagination, but I presume my night to be their industrious day, their fleeting hour of astute and obstinate existence.

I wake at dawn in a deserted and taciturn village, just as I had left it on the previous evening. Nothing has changed. I would like to recognize some trace of a life that had liberated itself while I slept, unleashed by my dreams; but everything is intact and dry, immune to any clue. I can fantasize that an extraordinary game has been played around me, that someone scrutinized my sleep, and that at the initial signs of my reawakening, everyone fled to that hiding place they have, of which I will never know anything, not even whether it exists.

I walk through the streets for the last time, like a tourist in a city he will never again visit. My steps are light and I exit at last through the gate in the palisade, without looking back; I return to the road and discover myself listening behind me to hear if there are traces of any voice at my shoulders—listening, in short, to hear if everything had only been awaiting my departure before re-taking possession of the places of life. I hear nothing. Before long I am too far away. I have to proceed. Slowly, as always.

Leaving the village behind me, I find that something in the structure of the road has changed. Everywhere I look I see not signs of erosion or things worn by use, but of something not yet complete: something initial and unperfected. Do I therefore admit that the road until now has shown some sort of perfection? Not at all. But the road I have walked was everything it might have been, and it enjoyed a kind of wholeness I no longer rediscover. There are nothing more than indications, but little by little as I proceed it strikes me that they thicken. The road is less compact; lengthy fissures appear and disappear. The terrain is grainy and consumed, as would happen in periods of sustained drought. I stop and examine these signs because the road, until now, had been clearly a candid and unsullied expanse, with never a trace of even an ironic inscription. I ask myself if these fissures bear meaning. Lazily—indolence has no minor role in the course of this itinerary—I investigate possible allusions. These illegible signs might furnish the theoretical silence of the village church with the documents of its subtle and enigmatic devotion. I necessarily wonder if there may not be a furor in the obscurity of these sores that blemish the itinerary, and whether these signs may not allude to an inevitable error, to a corruption, to a decadence of the path I walk and of my body as well—some deliquescence that in no way presupposes a moment of former corporeal harmony, no previous progress of accurate, well-marked rhythms. Perhaps the road is ill, infected with myself; or we are each reciprocal infection, reciprocal symptom; or perhaps while proceeding I have entered a naturally imperfect place; even a place of natural deformity, intrinsically inexact. The locus that I scan and travel, this road progressively more troubled by cracks and fragmentations, is an initial road, something in the throes of a birth, but to which a telos as road has perhaps forever been prohibited. So I approach a beginning, even if it is not clear that the beginning is the beginning of the road; I know only that what I approach is a place of the obscurely and intensely initial.

I see at a subsequent turning that the road has suddenly dilated, and that naked terrain is everywhere evident, as though some painstaking sketch for a path had been abandoned, or perhaps protracted and deferred. Nothing here appears demolished, though clearly distressed, perturbed and thrown into disarray along a route that had shown the qualities, no matter how illusory, of ordered and continuous coherence. More exactly: this thing I walk, no longer in any straight line, but chancing through constantly mutable widths and directions, is not a road at all; and it is slowly, increasingly losing its vocation even as itinerary. As I proceed, the terrain around me grows ever more corrupt, shaping itself into an extended fragment of a plain; and I realize that such a space—by now no more than that—can never contain provision for any sort of dwelling, neither villages, nor houses, nor even the crudest benches. Yet still the sensation persists that in some way or another I have simultaneously trod an itinerary toward an unknown ending and equally toward some beginning; that the earth I trample has something of the crumbled, grainy soil of a grave, and something as well of an abandoned construction site where a project has not ceased to linger. Is it not in fact a project, this thing I begin to discover at my feet? And is it not, this project, marred and corrupted by the decomposing, crumbling matter on which it spreads?

I am not amazed, but questioning; and I scrutinize the peremptory, scudding reddish lines that seem to trace an abstract map. Straight lines cover the clods of earth and scribe what appear to me to be squares and rectangles. If this is a map of a possible village, I am voyaging now among blueprints for walls; I pause near circles that might be fountains, or playground boxes of sand for equally intentional infants. A longish rectangle concludes in an apse: I wonder if I stand once again before a synoptic church. If these drawings—which appear to spread endlessly outwards, designing less a village than a city—embody an allusion to a structured possibility, I must then presume their inclusion as well, in no intelligible but still an imaginable way, of all the projected infant voices; and that somewhere there is a depot of dialogs, elsewhere a storehouse of births, and an arsenal of deaths, a powderhouse of rages and reconciliations. I suppose myself at the center of a possible infinity, such that no further progress is possible. Have I therefore arrived? But no matter where this point of arrival may be, it is surely no place that describes itself as meaning or goal. Or perhaps not only have I not arrived, but find myself in a place where a silent din of obstructed possibilities can only deny me all hope of a terminus: a hope I never truly nurtured but nonetheless envisioned as a somehow reasonable sequel to departures, abandonments, forfeits, confusions, and loss.

In the place where I presently find myself there is a mixed, ambiguous, and turbid quality that does not exactly command me to a standstill, but that stiffens me into an ancipital interrogation in which I know I might consume my slight eternity.

If I scumble the earth with my foot, I cannot avoid perceiving that this soil has been riddled by numberless encounters with things both living and totally consumed; and in the same space of time I perceive that nothing remains of any of them, not of anything at all, except a faint and doubtful imprint; yet this senescence of matter would still seem to find its contrast and abrogation in the brilliant, insistent coherency of the design I have defined as the project. But have I actually so defined it? If I turn my mind again to my words and fantasies, I realize that I have never truly conceived of this project as a point of departure for a future, or as possessing any intent towards being; I have never suspected that those voices, those births, those deaths, were at any moment on the verge of springing from their home in hypothesis. And puzzling now on this dark and rotted earth, I cannot escape another fantasy: that the drafted plan I see before me traces out the streets and buildings of a village, a metropolis—a distinction, at this point, which can hardly matter—that has always been extinct, its nonexistence, as well as its death, always included in these very signs that could have seemed to read as intentions of life and duration. Always extinct, I say, because the temporal quality of the end of this city is eternal, just as the future prospect of a city to be constructed can only be eternal. For this city to be infinitely projected into a future or infinitely buried within a past, both total, seems thus to make no difference. The quality of this unthinkable city is necessarily eternity. And how could I deny that I experience a certain sense of relief among these street designs and squares, among these indications of a superimposable future and past. I wonder who I myself may be in such a place, myself and the many houses, the rain, the village, the departures. I suspect that this village is my capital. I myself am drafted in blood-red chalk on the dead, crumbled earth. I am a project and equally the groundplan of myself. I know that if I lie upon the ground I will in no way be distinct from these mnemonic, projectural signs. I am dreaming myself: as happens in dreams, I am infinitely past and infinitely future. Dead since the beginning, I am always being born. I am the project.

The H Point

I find myself at a point I shall denominate H, since this letter knows no mode of pronunciation.* Let us further assume that other points be disposed around this H point, and I will call them A, B, and C. Setting out from point H in the direction of point A, I will cover a distance of two hundred farsangs before encountering a region of unblemished whiteness, lacking consistence, and vibrant with an utterly imprecise and opinable pulsation that emits a slight, constant whispering which likelihood suggests to be not devoid of meaning, but a meaning that I cannot decipher, nor would want to. This expanse of whiteness, which I presume to be asleep, though not soundly, since its murmuring might be substance exuded from a dream, is vast and impenetrable, owing not, however, to its offering resistance, but to its offering none at all. To explain

*Translator's Note: In the very rare cases where the letter "h" precedes a vowel in Italian words, or where it concludes a word after following a vowel, it is totally silent; otherwise, it appears exclusively for the purpose of indicating the hard pronunciation of the letters "c" and "g" where they occur before the vowels "e" or "i." A "c" or "g" directly before an "e" or an "i" is pronounced, respectively, as the English "ch" in "charity" or the "g" in "geometry." The interposition of an "h" between a "c" or "g" and a following "e" or "i," indicates that they are instead to be pronounced as in "caution" or "game."

exactly what I mean, I would return to the figure of sleep: should you attempt to traverse a zone of pure somnolence—meaning no somnolence of sleeping animals or plants, but purely sleep itself, unencumbered by any subject mired down within it—you would find yourself deprived of every mode of advance, your limbs being unadapted to effecting motion through sleep. Clearly, I myself have never advanced beyond the outmost border of this region, which I presume to be enormous even while supposing that it reaches no further than to a very great distance from point A. I will be asked if I have made no attempt to awaken this region of sleep. I reply that I have dared the experiment only once, and what occurred still disturbs me. For a moment, this great white space revealed itself to be rife with creatures of enormous violence: beings, no matter the conundrum, who were awake within the space of sleep; meaning, they were awake in sleep's interior and could only have been reached by its penetration. I will be asked if I ever attempted such a penetration, entering this sleep to become its proprietor and to establish rightful access to those wakeful beasts inside it. Yes, I have tried. But I had to retreat to escape an especially insidious metamorphosis: anyone who accepts an identity as sleep becomes entirely continuous with sleep; and though surely he can be inhabited by the beasts who live as wakeful denizens of sleep, he will find no possibility of drawing them into dialogue. Whoever comes to be occupied by these beasts—an inexact though hardly futile term—will never be relinquished, and though suffering no harm will know no further progress, neither forward nor backward. These beasts are in their own way affectionate, but not wholly free of treachery, and I have sometimes thought their existence analogous to the existence attributed to the dead. Surely I possess no exact information on the structure of point A, and indeed I cannot be certain of its existence: I know only that this barrier of drowsing whiteness encourages surmisal of a blocked itinerary, and thus the implication that beyond this space must lie a point of arrival. Why this obstacle has been erected in this place—if terming it a place is admissible—is something I could not say; but I assume that a metamorphosis into sleep, if I had the courage to permit it, would then comport my further transformation into one of those beasts I define as awake by virtue of their ubication in sleep's interior. I also imagine that sleep is the food of these beasts: I would be pasture for monsters, and nothing more. Or finally I might conjecture that this whiteness has cognition of point A and tolerates no one's approach, since for anyone to reach point A would determine that the place of sleep, the beasts, and the whiteness would serve no further purpose and thus be suppressed. From such an explanation, I could construe no characteristic of point A, if not that it stands closed off to the beasts within the barricade of somnolence, and perhaps that the beasts and point A are incompatible. Point A is certainly possessed of enormous beauty and dignity, and I see it as designed within something solid and compact, an acrid locale of fixed geometries. I wonder why I have called it "acrid." Perhaps for the pleasure in the use of a sharp and pungent word; or rather from the conviction that those beasts of sleep can be no less ferocious than simultaneously gentle, whereas certainly point A is neither, being instead an exact arrangement of forms devoted to the coherency of a mind intrinsic to that point itself. Point A is unacquainted with sleep, and no beast would dare approach it. I have frequently reflected that point A is indisputably onerous, even perhaps humanly impossible, but I wonder if what I seek can be anything other, precisely, than a form of human impossibility: something that disclaims my profile and surrounds my hands with doubt. It is not to be imagined that I strive for anything proud or superlative, but simply for something extraneous that does not know me, and which to me is unknown. I am aware of my imprecision, but find it not to be dictated by angst, spite, or nostalgia; it stems uniquely from my need to lose myself along an itinerary that is not an itinerary of sleep.

I ask myself whether point A may not be a city, depopulated but nonetheless perfect, a point where the world is totally organized and elevated to maturity. This city can display as many houses as I have desires, as many churches as the number of my faiths, as many tombs as my deaths. For in the moment of allowable access to that place, I would teem into a crowd and yet remain a dearth. I would know both solitude and promiscuity, dialogue and silence. It would always be dawn in some of the precincts of the city, others would glow with the constant light of one of the various hours of the evening and the night. One of its quarters would be in continual or alternating spring, another perpetually immersed in peaceful, claustrophobic winter. As crowd, my experience would be of simultaneous gamuts of feasts, vigils, sleeps, births, deaths, confessions and silences. Yet I cultivate no more than hypothesis on that point I call point A, deducing its form from the interposed obstacle of the whiteness, the sleep, the beasts alive inside the sleep. Giving myself a description of point A suffices to arouse the sensation of drawing deep and definitive breath. But point A remains unreachable.

The route from point H to point B is obstructed after approximately three hundred and twenty-two leagues by a teeming zone of numbers and geometric figures; together they form a kind of nebula, resplendent and arid, with which I establish no other relationship than fearful amazement. Depending upon the way I look at these numbers and figures, they assume the character of eyes, of fragments of faces, of sterile genitals, of models for increate beings. Attempting to advance in that direction, I realize the numbers and figures to cover an enormity of space, and its depth is such that I cannot discern its extremities. It would seem not impossible to traverse this space, but the numbers and images occupy and organize the void in a way congenial to them alone, and to nothing else. I wonder if these images are truthful, and I am forced to admit that they are perhaps endowed with life, but with a life that subtracts itself from all judgments of truth and falsehood. If I attentively scrutinize this space, I discern a three-cornered cloud, luminous and threatening, and then nebulae of hexagons, octagons, and other, irregular figures, all engraved in empty and perfect obscurity. Because this is to be noted: the space is dark, totally, and beyond the understanding of anyone who might desire to cross it; the light that wounds this darkness, while never dispersing it, finds its source in the numbers and figures of which I have spoken. But the power of that light is for them alone, and it is therefore not impossible, even if incomprehensible to me, for the threes to see or illumine the circles and isosceles triangles, and to be seen by them in turn. To me their nature seems only and entirely visual. But their light, from a technical viewpoint, has nothing to do with me, and I make out nothing at all between one light and another; and where this is no light, there is only darkness, a darkness which I suspect and fear to be solid, a form of space filled out with blind and compact substance that yields and assents only to the numbers' gelid glow. There is no question, then, of courage or ingenuity; the itinerary is objectively denied to me. I can proceed no further. The darkness does not stretch out as flat expanse before me, but stands erect as perpendicular impediment to my course. And even if this darkness were such as to come to terms with my hunger to advance, I know that the numbers and polygons have together created a world that belongs to them alone; I could enter this place only by accepting a transformation into number, or into drafted line. Since both possibilities are either denied to me or repugnant, I can only tell myself a fable around the theme of my metamorphosis into number: a number (to make it capable of passing unobserved in that world) that I imagine as greater than zero and less than one, yet not a fraction. It is clear that I dissimulate a useless cunning that knows no possible efficacy, and yet which offers consolation in the very moment that I understand there is nothing I can do. I have no way of proceeding, no way of transforming myself into numeral. I may be asked what I find so repugnant in such a transformation: first of all, the sensation that the numbers, luminous as they are, are intimately obscured by a lack of passional articulation. The three, for example, is blinded or dazzled by the passion of being three; and if grazed by any other passion, it is the passion of contiguity to triangular, hexagonal, or some similar type of form. Inward concentration on themselves as number deletes all possibility of their being anything other than number. It follows, too, that their world cannot accept any number that does not share this reflexivity, which in fact is proper to numbers.

I do not believe that this or any other form of concentration is proper to me; I have sought an existence as a creature of disorder, constantly on the hunt for myself. So for me there is no respite or opening in the world of numbers, which are ignorant of complicity or distraction—not by virtue of any sort of vigilance, but by virtue of infinite self-consistency.

All of this makes me wonder what this point can be, to which access is rendered impossible by interpositioned numbers. Certainly it must be incompatible with the world of number, and perhaps these worlds flee from and detest one another. I suppose it to follow that the articulation of point B is no less placid than extreme: a place capable of passion and distraction, intimately inexact, a place where life and death, wakefulness and sleep, color and absence of color habitually mix without ever giving rise to any unseemly fracture, any internal passion prone to move in two incompatible directions. I might suppose point B to resemble a giant body, alive with innumerable lives and perhaps discontinuous, even though surely inapt for definition as vegetable, animal, human, or crystalline. But we can suppose it slow and peaceable like the vegetable world, impetuous and cunning like the animal, full of fantasy and logic like the human, frank and taciturn like crystal. It courses with dark, disruptive drives of love and hate: love that bestows a part of its being on something else, and that reduces a part of something else to itself. But this love and hate never conflict with or stand in opposition to one another, and point B finds contentment both in its self-love and self-hatred. Point B is aggressive, let's say, with a part of itself that we can define, for ease of narration, as the left; but its right-hand part is peaceful, conciliatory, and comprehending. These two parts can thus encounter and recognize one another as reciprocally necessary. One part is enticed by the theme of its death, but is kept alive by the other, which is a constant discourse on the worth of life; and this other is moored to awareness of death by the part which death fascinates and seduces. If point B were capable of lust, it would nonetheless remain chaste; if it could kill, it would still remain unwoundable; if it could dream, it would be uninterruptedly awake. The space this being occupies is tendentially unlimited; but the being itself is both limited and borderless. It ceaselessly proceeds and ceaselessly halts; it rests and precipitously runs; it is infinitely deep and infinitely superficial; it is noble and shameful. Finally, it both is and is not.

I think it right to imagine that this contradictory and fragmentary mode of being is intolerable to the world of numbers; and that these numbers in fact have been posted here to damn all consciousness of point B into oblivion, reducing it to mere phantom and hypothesis. Something without credibility. The numbers know that the world must either belong to them or to that other and intimately impossible creature: this something which it is not possible to count, nor even to describe with an uninterrupted graphic sign, no matter whether sharply cornered or shaping a perfect circle. Somehow or another, two forms of perfection stand opposed to one another: one perfection that knows itself, and therefore perfect; another perfection that negates, interrupts, and lacerates itself, and therefore imperfect. Whatever an imperfect perfection might be I could not conceptually define; yet I can somehow comprehend it, considering how my face (and I am only a face) oscillates between perfect imperfection and imperfect imperfection. And still I consider it proper, and not insidious, for a desert of numbers to divide me from what I cannot know and put into practice: an imperfect perfection: a perfection that could only be inferior to itself were it not imperfect.

An excursion from point H in the direction of point C brings me after a march of eighty-seven days to an entirely specific obstacle, meaning a barrier I would never dare imagine to find anywhere else. This obstacle is an enormous gulf, or rather a total absence of universe. Still, it has dimensions, even though it is not possible to measure them, and likewise impossible (as would be the case with measurable things) ever to reach the bottom of it. Were I to penetrate this absence of being, I would meet no more than a beginning of nothingness, which as such would have no choice but every time to rebegin again. Nullity has no parts, comes to no end, has no middle; everywhere that I would find myself, I would be always at the beginning, at the center, at the end. And still this infinitely precipitous place is governed by this contradiction: that it does not occupy the whole of the universe—I myself am proof; and that even though logical necessity declares it finite, I inhabit it as an infinity. It is obvious that the verb "to inhabit" is wholly mental and indicative of nothing real; because this void is uninhabitable: uninhabitable not by virtue of prohibition but rather by such total acquiescence as to negate compatibility with any and all mode of subsistency. It has all the characteristics of an infinity, and yet I have no choice than to suppose it finite. But how can something be finite when by definition it has neither beginning nor end? In reality, the disturbing question is not to ask why a lacunary place of total absence should exist on the path from point H to point C: I find this absence to be totally reasonable and rational, and of a consistency I in no way dare to challenge. What leaves me amazed is that something exists outside of that void, since there is no exception to nothingness, by virtue of its very character as exception, that can be exempt from an act of prevarication that participates in error and infraction. In short, what amazes me in the face of this lacuna is the fact that I exist; and I cannot help thinking of my existence as blasphemous and wretched, since it raises an objection to the factuality of this perfect absence. This then is the feeling to which this constantly self-regenerative obstacle excites me: amazement at myself. If I dared to enter the lacuna—which sometimes I have imagined to do, sketching out feeble projects—it is possible that the gulf might appear to have been abolished. This is to say that if I advanced beyond the edge of the abyss I would still not enter it, because the extent of my penetration would exactly correspond to the distance by which the lacuna would itself withdraw. I would always be at its border, and always incapable of going beyond into what is not there. But let us suppose I might be just sufficiently ignored—certainly not accepted—to allow first entrance; I tell myself that then I would become an exception, a discontinuity, an error enveloped inside of something which is rule, completeness, and exactitude. Since the lacuna has no beginning, middle or end, I myself would be beginning, middle and end; the void would begin in me, surround me, and in me would have its conclusion. Having all the rational characteristics of infinity, the lacuna would in no way come to be modified, nor have to recede before me; it would simply take no account of me. This much is certain: I would be an object neither of acceptance nor rejection; and while ignoring me—which is all it could do—the lacuna would attribute to me the qualities of a different but in its own way homogeneous lacuna. So I would take on the character of an absence inside of absence, but one not subject to assimilation, even if logic again would dictate that lacuna must display no qualitative differentiations. The lacuna and myself would become a contradiction, while yet an identity: both lacunae; both unknown and unknowing; both absence, but two absences; both interrelated and discontinuous; and both of us would participate in nullity even though our access to this nullity would find its points of departure along reciprocally extraneous paths. And even if I abstain from any attempt to overcome this continuous discontinuity, even if I make no attempt to infringe upon it, nonetheless I locate myself in an advantageous and extremely disturbing position. I have every reason to be convinced that the void can ignore what lies within it— even if it has no "within"—but I am far from equally certain that it does not clash with everything that lies outside of it. If I linger outside of this place of absence, my quality as error grows enormous and invasive and becomes a challenge as well: I am the beginning, the middle, I am the end. If the whole of the universe, the existence of which I suppose, were mere hallucination in no way endowed with the power to corrupt the integrity of this crater, I, the hallucinator, remain always that monstrous and unsoundable exception to the void, of which the void has no choice but to take recognition, and which it can deny but not ignore, even if nothing that it knows is not itself. But look at what I have said: the very self of which the lacuna is aware is what comes to be altered by the fact of my existence: by the hallucinator, the error, the discontinuous discontinuity. The only way to address this void is thus to look at the void and to say to him—this pronoun amuses me—"You are absence, but I, no matter how illogically, am not absence, not in any way at all." So finally it would be the task of nothingness to cross through me, and not vice versa. . . . But there is nothing that nothing can traverse except at the cost of self-annihilation. And this nullification of nullibeity, though linguistically impeccable, presents itself as an utterly irreparable solution, and above all else as an undoing of nothingness, which is linguistically impossible. So this is our condition: we are unrelated and consanguineous, matrices of reciprocal destruction coupled together in non-being. All we can do is to measure one another, even if for separate reasons we are each incommensurable; we are reciprocal pitfall and reciprocal destiny, each to the other; we are a taciturn dialogue of opposing lacunae, reasons and unreasons, and as such we endure.

This logically rigorous but in other ways impossible situation presents a question: the question as to what can be the nature of this C point that is thus denied to me. Supposing the obstacle to deploy itself in negative accord with the point to which I would wish to arrive—though the term "would wish" is improper—I must imagine point C to be something totally opposed to lacuna: some compendium of the universe, a total crystal, without introit, preamble, fissures or recesses. Point C must, likewise, be no less inaccessible than the void. But it is totally existent, and we therefore have a family relationship; or, rather, I know myself to partake of the selfsame category, even if our difference is such as can only confound all attempts at communication. I have said that I see point C as consisting totally and exclusively of reality. Which means that, unlike me, it is immune to all change, beginning, end, or dialectic; it neither desires nor detests, neither wants nor rejects, and it is not wrathful even if it is not meek. I do not know if it can be reasonable to affirm that I feel a kind of love for point C. Perhaps the term is inexact. Truthfully, I know nothing about point C that could make it worthy of love, or in any case an object of love. Firstly, I am ignorant as to whether it has a form, since a form implies limits, or a confine. But as absolute contrast to the void, the point of total reality has in common with the void an utter unthinkability of confines, limits, or places where it ceases to be reality. Yet I know from experience that reality and lacuna coexist, and I should therefore infer that lacuna makes a halt where reality establishes a beginning. Or, that reality presses forward to where it brushes the periphery of lacuna. But supposing as well that neither lacuna nor reality shows fractures or discontinuities, limits or conclusion, I face a situation surely to be called extreme. Since reality and lacuna ought to meet, and since I am not lacuna, I ought, being reality, to experience lacuna as a place of existence concomitant with the real. And there is more: if reality is the reality of point C, I myself—I myself being real, and the point of reality experiencing no real terminus—cannot really be discontinuous with point C. I would thus be forced to conclude that I am myself point C, and not so much a part of point C than rather point C pure and simple; and what I have spoken of as fractures would not be real and might indeed be classed either as acts of cowardice that I myself have committed with respect to the real, or as acts of assent with respect to lacuna, this lacuna which continually flows into me, or with which I entertain an obscure form of commerce. But should this second hypothesis be true, I would be less point C than a mediation between point C and the lacuna, participating in both: by virtue of the lacuna I am capable of loving C, and I am capable by virtue of C of taking flight from the lacuna. I find it clear that the modes for describing the terms of this perigrination—myself, lacuna, point C—are extremely obscure; and the condition in which each of these three places comes to find itself is surely no less obscure, even if it has to be clear that lacuna is in its own particular way oblivious to clarity, as point C is to obscurity. The only remaining conclusion is that I, and I alone, am the problem, the clarity, and the obscurity of the itinerary. Even if I hold the certainty that I cannot reach point C, I am also certain of not being alien to that point, since, thanks to its totality as realness, it is my natural unit of measure; and again there can be no doubt—even if I dare not repeat the hypothesis of being a part of point C—that only the putative yet cogent existence of point C prevents me from being continuous with lacuna. Point C is therefore necessary, and constitutes my foundation; but somehow or another I could never dare renounce my awareness of lacuna, since it is owing to my discontinuity, mimed on the structure of lacuna, that I have the possibility of recognizing point C as an element of my own inherency, example and incantation. It follows that if this absence did not exist, I could not desire to reach point C. The obstacle is the journey's premise, absence conducting towards totality, dearth signalling the route to plenitude. The whole of the progress is itself both immobile and in movement: myself, lacuna, and point C are respectively traveller, wayside stop, and point of arrival. But they are also immobility, impossibility, uncrossability. As I move, the measure of the real repeats to me that I stand immobile, traversing no space; but lacunary cunning advises me that I cannot not advance and must be ever closer, though always no less distant from the conclusion of my itinerary. I can affirm with absolute certainty that only the presence of absence assures me that this is the route towards C, that only the hypothesis of C gives certainty that the lacunary void is essential and total, and that finally only the coincidence of C and lacuna makes it possible to posit my image as both of a lacunal being and of a real being, as in transit and as never approaching: always at the same unmeasurable, non-quantitative, but qualitative distance from the conclusion of my voyage.

The description of my situation as a voyager from point H to points A, B, and C would now, at this juncture, seem clear and conclusive; yet I would hardly be honest if I made no mention of other interpretations of the situation in which I surmise to find myself. Factually put, the existence of points A, B, and C is entirely deductive and in every case hinges on the existence of an obstacle that I judge to have challenged my course. The specific qualities of these three points are likewise the fruit of perhaps unfounded deductions I have drawn from the typifying qualities of these impediments. But even allowing the existence of these three points, I have no proper way, rigorously speaking, to consider the impediments as actually corresponding to any such definition of themselves: surely they are hostile elements, but they might have been called into play by the terminal points themselves, out of a desire to be pursued but never reached. And to reach the limits imposed by the impediments—the whiteness, the numbers, the lacuna—would be tantamount already to achieving the goal, my inability for all further progress being determined by the goals themselves. In that case, I could be said to experience the negatives of my objectives, having reached them in the form of their refusal to be reached. In that case, my itinerary is crowned with success, even if that success takes the form of its defeat. Perhaps there is no other way of concluding so long an itinerary, and I have brought it already to an end. Even supposing that points A, B, and C do not exist, I would find myself in a situation to be defined, somehow, as privileged. The final virtues of these three points would have to be recognized in the places I have termed "impediments." And there is more. It is not impossible for a shift to have taken place, by reason of which the impediment of whiteness would be nothing other than point B, the mathematical impediment would be C, and the lacuna would be A. No impediment would actually exist, but it would come about that one pursues point A by directing oneself towards C, and indeed thus reaches it. Likewise for the other points. Each of the points, merely by the voyager's equivocations, would become something he uses as impediment to the reaching of the point elected as truly necessary and goal. The fiction of impediments would come to be abolished, replaced by a system where the points are so arranged that the voyager pursues them through modes of alternativity, transforming each into impediment to the reaching of another; and this case, which strikes me as conceitfully subtle, would lead to concluding that each of the points is by nature unreachable but nonetheless reached, but only and always on condition of error. So in every case I arrive, while remaining incapable of any such realization. And on arriving at each of these points, I consider it an error, simply from ignorance of its pertinence and specificity. Only through error am I right.

Finally, for purely mental game, I prospect a final fable: I am not the voyager, and I proceed in no direction; and my discourse on themes of itinerary is only a crafty ploy for attracting points A, B, and C, inviting them to move in my own direction so that they, and not I, will have to pose and resolve the problem of the impediments, which extends beyond my own capabilities. So points A, B, and C are the travellers, and it is I, the inhabitant of point H, who am the goal; but with the simple, obvious hitch, since I posit myself as having departed, that point H does not exist.

System

The system consists firstly of the Fires, which, numbering from two to seven, inhabit, pervade, and characterize the central space; hence, they are also known as Essences. The Fires or Essences are bound to no necessitated movements; indifferently, they sometimes travel with regularity, not rarely in circles, at other times in accordance with irregular and unpredictable patterns, and often they remain in total immobility. The Essences are distinguished by no established or definite form; their noetic model would seem to be the sphere, though none display that attitude precisely, deviating into various flaws: there are Essences flattened at the poles, or oblong, or roundish but jaggedly pitted, and some are even so artfully deformed as to make them seem plagued by some type of infirmity. It can be added that the form of an Essence, independent of its momentary shape, is always unstable; and at times a transaction takes place in which two or more Essences will barter and exchange their forms. Essences in any and all systems, moreover, will not infrequently cluster, adhere to and impact with one another, such that two, or three, or even seven, if so many are present, can outwardly assume the guise of but a single unitary Fire. This radical condition where all of the Fires conjoin into a sole collaborative Essence is extremely rare, and perhaps it signals a blight with which the whole of the system is incurably afflicted. When all the Fires contract into a single Fire, they nullify that state of alacrid discord where each can course through countless changing designs while engaging in mutual, inter-relational discourse. These Essences, in fact, are different from one another, and even reciprocally incompatible; on welding into apparent singularity, they accordingly emanate conflicting Lights. By Lights, I refer to the messages, no matter their nature, which Essences broadcast around them. So the condition they experience in clusters is not infrequently anguished, always onerous and fictively affectionate, intimately irate. The dispersal of such unchosen concourse will signal its utter dissolution, the Fires then fleeing to great distances, at times so enormous that further conversation becomes for a while impossible between one Fire and another. This state will endure until the straits of cohabited contradiction have been forgotten. But since the Fires appear unable to pass a given confine, their resumption of what we term their conversation is, eventually, a matter of course. The intercourse of the Essences is slow, circumspect, precious, and prudent for the greater part of the time, but not unoccasionally it tends towards hostility, or at least to acrimony, though never to violence. The Fires converse through modifications of their shapes, when possible, and by altering the paths of the Lights. When ill or decrepit, Essences are incapable of changing shape and are trapped within the single form that afflicts them; Lights are then to be classed as Moans. But an Essence resides when ill in a peripheral space and has no others with which to discourse.

It is nonetheless impossible for an Essence to die. An Essence afflicted by clearly eternal infirmity—eternal by deathless incurability—will thus be cause for a brief, intense agglomeration in which the languishing Fire is embraced by all the other Fires, then to be redistributed in some unclear way among them, these others being still intact. The sickly Essence thereupon dissolves; and its infirmity, equably parcelled among those that remain, will show as a welt on one of them, a protuberance on another, or as frost intermixed with the fire of a Fire, or again as filaments of liquid aerial filth that the Essences trail behind them in the devolution of their courses. The lexicon of the extinguished Fire is shared and divided, meaning it not to be mistakenly declared that the illness, subsequent dismemberment, and then redistribution of an Essence is enrichment for the intercourse of the Essences that remain: their intricate dialogue finds flavoring spice in the acrid humors of the sores, the cunning purulence, the pathetic clottings, the fetid melodic exhalations, and finally of the festered ashes of the Fire that has found itself consumed.

No Fire can prevail upon the others. There is no such occurrence as subordination, no centripetal devotion. Clusterings take place by happenstance, and need not be unique; it will be rather that three Fires, here or there, will mingle and hold each other company while two residual Fires will elsewhere continue to transit on solitary and perhaps alarmed itineraries. We have here supposed a system of seven Fires; but systems, as previously stated, may be composed of from two to seven, never of one, if not on these occasions of a perilous promiscuity of maleficent, intermingling ardors.

Essences are endowed with internal transparency, making it feasible to subject them to scrutiny; but the clarity that swamps their interior is extreme and deliquescent, and subtly blinding: intimate shadows seem glimpsed in the guise of declivities and high plateaus, but one's eyes in fact stand beguiled by episodes of rapid, staccato vertigo. Since they are Fires, one sees nothing of the Essences but the irate fingerings of their flame, the haughtiness of a fulgence intolerant of investigation. But with this to be added: that since they are Fires they show no certain possession of any center ulterior to the act of inexhausted self-consumption into a high, demanding ardor; their existence as Fire thus seems to feed only on prior Fire, which in turn devours the Intimate; the whole of their existence would be only as Fire, and thus with neither hope nor harbored expectation of extinguishment, nor for attenuated heat. This Fire is Fury, and only monologue can issue from within it: monologue intent on constant commission of diseased locutions, no less rife with plague than with wisdom. But Fires likewise exist as Essences; and as Essences they hover in a state of fictive clarity, illusory distinctness. And what was uncontainable ardor as a Fire is as Essence a vitreous cold and a genteel germination of flashing lights. The outline of an Essence is sharp and geometric, and Essences never converse if not through rapid silences, exquisite laconicisms, ellipses and lacunae that intersperse among the avid, burning cracklings of the Fires. The interior depth of an Essence is unsoundable, if an Essence be possessed of an interior: unsoundable because Essence is nothing else than Essence, though nonetheless scarified, gouged, and flayed through its actions upon itself.

But what finds denomination as Fire or Essence can posit itself equally as Center, which exists first of all as its intimate intention to sphericality. Center, as mentioned before, can never take the form of a present and manifest sphere, but it configures a state of steadfast inquiry into achievement of sphericality. Therefore its quality of utter and unapproachable striving, a loftiness intolerant of all investigation; Center likewise knows no contentment, spurning all compassion; and not seldom scowling, perceiving a surrounding ubiquity of adversarial faces. The Centers are vessels of power, and hold the will and government of the things of the system. Reciprocally intent upon ignoring one another, they direct their gaze uniquely towards the system, which they administer no less than afflict; their mode of existence ponderous and intolerable both to others and to themselves. One draws no intelligence from the motions of the Centers, their majesty admitting of no indiscretions.

These Fires, or Essences, or Centers have a final mode of existence whereby we speak of Edified Beasts: referring to their endowment with the image of the Beast that wheels and flees and pursues, but a Beast appearing in no way to be made of flesh; rather that the burning of Fire, the crystal of Essence, and the effort of Center all minister to the Edification of the Beast, which is a constructed thing, though of no material other than itself. As Beast, it is also agent and victim of atrocious pain; the Edified Beast rears up in its height as animate and disemboweled, a blooded out-splayed gut. This blood flows outwards and distends into space, and seethes and coagulates, which is perhaps the mode of discourse most properly allowable to such metamorphic Fires. Eviscerated, quartered, and eternal, the Edified Beasts hide nothing of the mystery of their bowels; but these bowels, though evident and even lapidary, are unamenable to interpellation or augury; and their obscurity is an agony to the Edified Beasts. One might desire to know what beasts the Edified Beasts resemble; and one might be told that in pursuit they show the nature of the wolf; while as victims drained bloodless by wolfish teeth they are equally of the nature of the deer. They resemble the deer again as monarchs crowned with racks of horn; and again the wolf as creatures of solitude, crazed with caution. Other metamorphoses will perhaps be revealed in the parts of our discourse to follow.

Since this Edified Beast, imputably, is the most obscure of the metamorphoses of Fire, Essence and Center, it will not seem useless to examine it slightly further. The Beast is edified with the selfsame materials employed in the raising of palaces, prisons, temples and churches: material both organic and stoney: celestially sacred: infernally consecrated, desecrated and deconsecrated, and sacred again. More to be classed as showing multiplicity than as self-contradictory, this material is itself the secret of how a Beast both wolf and deer can be constructed and birthed from it. As wolf the Beast pursues, hides diffident in its lair, and forays out on silent feet. As deer it is agonized prey and monarch incoronate with a crown of bone. It therefore will not seem strange for the Edified Beast to know a still further transformation. From out of the Edified Beast, the Throne proceeds, but purely as untouched potential for royal repose, and therefor subject to no investigation: for the Throne is equally solemn and empty. Unlike Essences and Centers, Thrones engage in no form of dialogue at all; they seem even to enjoy no lexicon, neither for voicing intimidation nor articulating ceremony. If a Throne reflects on itself as Essence or Fire, it then consumes and exhausts itself: if as Essence, in a waning of light that nonetheless will never fade totally out; if as Fire, by enflaming itself into a rapid but never exhausted pyre. But should it think of itself as Center, it will split and grow ill, since it cannot attack while at once maintaining its motionless sublimity. The ailing Throne resists with all the power of senescence; for should it transmute into unassertive Essence, it will find itself consumed within a cluster of other Essences. Thronopathy is indeed much relished by the Essences. This then leads to mention of the most extreme metamorphosis of Fires or Essences or Centers or Edified Beasts or Thrones: their assumption of the indescribable forms of Thunders, whereby a lattice of rumbling darkness exerts its power on the system; their form as Shadow, accompanied by no intervening body nor by any sun, and uniquely comprehensible as a mode of dementia, cautious and sapid; their form as Memory, wherein all active power is supplanted by the simple persistence of a power that acted in an obstinate but not emendable past; their form as Prophecy, exercising power from some place of futurability which is always future and therefore never commensurable, just as the past is incommensurate, each reflecting the other as forever unattainable. The existence of a presence to be signalled as Nullity and Void is matter for exploration; but the impossibility of any such exploration appears to suggest that Void is, yes, a reasonable and possible form, and that all ulterior conclusions are perhaps foreclosed. Yet some maintain that Void can appear in two isomorphic forms: Void as absence, and Void as abolition, meaning as denial, negation, cancellation, recalcitrance; as No.

II

A system is to be understood as the whole of the locus—its dimensions irrelevant—holding custody of a region, or hub-like arena, or recess, or sky, which in turn is theater for the actions of those diverse guises and attitudes of what here have been termed sometimes as Fires, sometimes as Essences, or likewise Centers, and manifold Edified Beasts, and finally Thunders, Shadows and No, this last distinguishing, to form the final dyad, into No as vacuity and No as abolition. These Fires, or however else they manifest, move and remain at rest, hold silence and converse, pursue and flee, designing diverse signs as they act and dance sometimes in concert, sometimes in discord; nor is there any lack of gestures of threat and hostility, beginnings of brawls, or tacit affronts; further indication has been given that the Fires, or whatever else their form, will on occasion coalesce, whereby the hub will appear to depopulate, if only momentarily, then to mill yet again, shortly afterwards, with coursings of restless figures. This is the center of the system.

This center, as we have termed it—always unstable and rancorous—is next to be seen as pivot and focus for the comings and goings of what we speak of now as Places. Places have none of the qualities thought proper to the Fires or any other modes of the regal populace at the system's center, showing them not so much as even a vitiated, impoverished, or imitational resemblance. The Places differ from one another as well, and so greatly as to make themselves unsortable into any reasoned continuity. Even their movements differ, and have only this in common: that they attune to the actions presently taking place in the hub. Their state of motion is therefore irregular; yet even this has no constancy, meaning that any two Places show unlike reactions to the central hub's disorder. Systems include from nine to eighteen Places; since the Places are heterogeneous, there are no phenomena of coalescence; but resultant from the concourse of the denizens of the hub, the Places are known not seldom to undergo transformations.

Here we describe a system of twelve Places, judging it a reasonable number, easily surveyed and not overly crowded. We will first supply an entirely summary account, taking no heed of the sundry forms of obedience that Places will show to their hubs. Place one is an open Hand, the five fingers extended, conferring an attitude of supplication or cordiality; the Hand is truncated at the wrist; its tendential motion is elliptical; it displays neither signs nor ornaments, and cannot be determined as masculine or feminine; the fingers move slightly, retracting and extending, quite calmly. Four of the fingers sometimes fold inwards, and the index finger will for a while emerge: an inane and melancholy imperative.

The second Place to be described is an equilateral Triangle, the sides of which, however, rather than straight, are curved. A contorted image of a mouth has been drafted at its midpoint: incomplete, but not without a rudiment of a serpentesque tongue, which seems at times to attempt to tremble into a quivering patter or hiss. The motions of this arc-sided triangle are always disorderly, almost as though bickering with some other phantom and gripped at once by rage and fear; it is not beyond likelihood that its outward-pressing barbs express a will to puncture or scratch. The Triangle is prudently considered to be a skittish Place, unlovable and perhaps forlorn.

We have spoken of the Triangle's ability and perhaps imputable desire to wreak damage on some other phantom: this Phantom is the third of the Places our discourse considers. It is a fluttering blot of shadow and light, mutable and unstable as it shifts from one to the other, and it seems endowed with no other dimension than a single surface: but a surface as though ruffled by uninterrupted wind. The Phantom is not quarrelsome, and seems rather to be frightened, exhausted, and pained. It is frightened by the Triangle, and if intertwining trajectories sometimes bring it adjacent to the Hand, it will beseech a sort of benediction, an endearment, a not-hostile game of fingers that linger about it, shaping themselves into cradle and discontinuous home, or caressing and esteeming it between thumb and index, as though taking it for a cloth of woven shadow, and nothing more.

The Wind already will have been presumed to constitute the fourth Place, and is typified by a capricious though not malevolent course; always gusty, boisterous, and ready to thicken into episodes of spiteful if infantile affliction; or to spread into playful dissimulation of a sail; or to curl and tangle, an almost cirrus-like breeze; or to plummet and wholly to engulf itself, pretending a vortex of hilarity and aggression, a game of marine irascibility with swells and breakers and rapid eddies; quick and childish, it sometimes makes itself gusty, circling and scudding, spinning itself as its own toy top. Friends with the Phantom and detached toward the Triangle, it loves to lick against the fingertips of the severed Hand, languidly and with bashful haste; nor perhaps is the Hand ungrateful.

Place five is a Mere of brackish water, an irregular circle, but with no circumscription of any beach or shore. The Mere presses outwards until drawing this somewhat childish form to completion. The lack of any constant unit of measure permits no statement as to whether this puddle is in truth an ocean or a trifling splatter of mud; or whether beneath it lies a space making it more than a veil of humescence. The shape of this tarn is between that of an eye and a navel, or like a circle compassed by a child. This is the Place of quiet, or perhaps of defeated and afflicted remissiveness. It is skillfully playful if the Wind Place ruffles it, but its game is brief and cautious, like an infant conscious of its slightness, and perhaps distempered. The Mere hosts no form of animal, but soft slow algae sometimes sop within it, though to a depth that remains unknown, quickly reemerging to shake itself dry and then to evanesce.

Such Algae is thus Place six. Supremely unstable, it roils backwards from any proximity to any other Place even though it bears no mark of intrinsic impatience, no tendency to swagger. It barters a grave and measured breeze from the Wind; it is rootless and thus takes flight with no hint of resistance. Vegetable pinguitude gives it harbor from Triangular rancors. It briefly bathes in the Mere; it slithers up to the Hand, entwining it, seeking and finding repose between fingers and palm. The Algae and the Phantom converse like distant relatives, not unapprised of one another's lives; prone to languor, the Algae is fond of dallying in the presence of the tender, trembling Phantom. It measures its size against that of the Hand. But it cannot be determined that the Hand has only a single size, and it follows that the Algae's dimensions are various and discontinuous. Perhaps it corresponds to what we might call a "milky way"; it is perhaps an invisible, mucilaginous necklace of submarine verdure. It sometimes ties itself in knots, but easily loosens itself, nor does it tolerate constrictions that would hamper its volatile course as an imprecise creature of the air. The Triangle subjects it to scrutiny without apprehension, its rancor melting into dubious stupefaction. The Algae pacifies, though it knows no peace.

Place seven is the Ring: a yellowish circle inscribed with an indecipherable text. Could one read it, one might find names and a date. It is not unfeasible that the Ring may have slipped itself from the Hand already described. But at times the array of Places will also count the presence of a single, isolated and soliloquizing Finger of which the Ring might be in pursuit, or it in pursuit of the

Ring. This Finger, as just implied, is a Place of only occasional appearance; some Places are in fact unstable and seem not to number in the fixed and continuous series towards which they advance and likewise from which they retreat. These secondary Places seem connected through relations of dependency to the Places of the system, if not through relations of infatuated love. There is, therefore, no lack of exactitude in speaking of microsystems where continuous Places act as arena and central orientation for the secondary Places. The Finger, a secondary Place, thus orbits about the Ring; or Finger and Ring perhaps will sometimes orbit and at other times distance; there is no doubt that the Ring persists whereas the Finger is often in total eclipse. But Ring and Finger are never united; nor is conjecture allowed as to whether the Finger is part of a hand which pairs to the Hand that forms Place one, or of any other hand, either related or extraneous. It can be maintained with some certainty that the Finger's dominant affect is inexactitude; ground is less certain for supposing the Ring to pretend to a status as target.

Place eight is Light, meaning clarity with no apparent gift of form or consistency, neither objecthood nor animated substance: mere, unintelligible light. Light shows movements of perennial flux, oscillating and flaring, and its motion might indicate a predisposition to hilarity were it not for insistent suspicions that this Light is nocturnal, for the dispersal of shadows. Even having subtracted itself, or been subtracted, from the reign of night, it is nonetheless imbued with night, justified by night, held sacred by night. While sojourning in a space that is not night, its presence alludes to night and stands as indication of night, a nocturnal convocation. This Light, were it not for the blinding glare that hampers distinguishing its form, might be termed a luminous bat, and its shudders and tremors might stand in proxy for the slanting, starting flights sketched out by bats in the bristling obscurity of caverns. We can speak of this light-bodied bat as a reticent witness of darkness.

Place nine is an expanse of Beach watered by no sea. Dull brown sands unacquainted with life and offering no welcome to shattered rocks, worn pebbles, or the dusts of inanimate meteors. This is a place of patient, unlettered sadness, possibly indifference; we cannot be precise, since we are ignorant of how this Beach relates to the non-existent sea. There are no indications of a sea as a secondary Place; the meteors, on the other hand, most certainly exist but seem not to reach or strike the Beach; their birth and combustion were perhaps coeval, or they never achieve the shattering peace of precipitation. The Beach has no memory and no hope of the sea, no obsession with any project for a sea; and it is conceivably extraneous even to the concept of a sea, or at any rate of waves, no matter if fluvial or lacustrine or of any other body of water; yet this is doubtless and factually a beach and no simple desert. In its quality as Beach, it knows some mode of connection with at least the hypothesis of water; and it cannot be precluded that crisscrossed paths of Beach and Mere may have occasioned sufficient propinquity for each to shape some image of coherent reciprocity with the other. But this is hypothesis; the Beach may just as well be endowed with an exclusively nominal cognizance of the sea, and have need of nothing more.

Tenth Place is a female Sex, a slit or aperture in space; but so wholly and only aperture as to expose no trace of delimiting lips; it is thus an orifice, and gives ceaseless issue to eructations that conference themselves as secondary Places: a great waving banner; bottles of ink; guillotines; a fingerless nail; innumerable shadows thrown by no objects; a dead snake; a frozen cold. This invisible, concrete, untouchable and carnal Sex shows no apparent contact with anything that fecundates; there is no knowledge of semen as a secondary Place. This abstract female vent is thus imagined to enfold a uterus that generates purely from the will to generation; or perhaps the ovary is governed by the will of the Centers, or made gravid by the ardor of the Fires; and one might conjecture finally that the malady of the Fires is perhaps a venereal affliction stemming from congress with this volatile vagina. Since it is judged to be infectious, though by cause of no improper commerce, and by virtue alone of inborn self-rancor; since it is fertile yet free from contact with any agency that fecundates. It follows that no dialogue precedes its uninterrupted birthing.

The eleventh of the Places is the Ideogram, though it will be vain to ask of what, or in what mode, language, sermon or code. There is no doubt, however, that this Ideogram is a significant Place, even despite our eternal and inescapable ignorance of what and how it signifies. It even may be improper to speak of it as ideogram; nonetheless it is a careful and intricate interweaving of signs and designs, varyingly inclined and extending through enormities of space that no one could ever aspire to measure. The meander is uninterrupted, and the Ideogram may give expression, arguably, to more than some single or only several words; nothing disputes the feasibility of its being a complete and meticulous discourse: a perfect description, with notes and codicils, postilla and marginalia; rectifications and calculations; glosses and summaries; and perhaps it includes the grammar of itself and as well the rules of its syntax; and perhaps this grammar of the Ideogram—or of the total language the Ideogram incarnates—is nothing less than the mode through which the Ideogram functions. And if the Ideogram, as one supposes, is the description of the system—one seeing nothing else it might explain—it follows that the grammar of the Ideogram is the system's mode of being; and that the system itself is ideogram. There is no surprise in noting that secondary Places orbit about the Ideogram, and as follows: comma, parenthesis, paragraphings, capitalizations of absent letters, and above all an ample, desolate margin that vainly proposes itself as host to the Ideogram's precious majesty.

The Ideogram would be the system's point of maximum obscurity and maximum rationality, were it not succeeded by the Place of Collapse, which is less an abyss than pure precipitation—and less the action than the verb, there being some mode of relation between Collapse and the Ideogram. Collapse is silent and free of bloodshed; but uninterrupted, unexhausted, always unconcluded. Were the Places on one or another occasion to dispose themselves in compact sequence, and should the Thrones assent, the whole of the system might conceivably transform into collapse, couching itself as the verb "precipitate." The verb of Collapse is taciturn; it is unpronounceable, though a phoneme; though a verb, it is always in the infinitive and never conjugatable; though a word it is ignorant of lips and tongue, even if the secondary Places indisputably include a solitary Lip that vainly attempts throughout millennia to pronounce it, aware if it as the only thinkable verb.

III

It was said: "Should the Thrones consent." Fires, Essences and Thrones act upon the Places, and these upon the secondary Places; everything wheels and passes, grows intricate and disperses, designing ideograms, miming meres, rings, fingers, and hands; through the action of the indiscretion of the Fires, the oratory of the Center, the languor of the Essences, the contradictions of the Edified Beasts, the vacancy of the Thrones, the serenity of the Thunders, the seemliness of the absentious Void, the "?" of the abolishing Void, and finally the assent of the No, the system is transformed into each: meaning that in each respective case the whole of the system is only hand or mere or whatever else; and in conclusion everything tends towards ideogram and drafts its contours; we thus understand how the Ideogram is the system's symbol as well as its project; and how the system, finally, having made itself utterly Ideogram, finds the tacit consent of its Fires and everything else, and pronounces the verb "precipitate."

Of all the Places, it is only the Ideogram and the verb Precipitate that, in truth, excite no zeal in the central hub. The Fires, Essences, Centers, Thrones and the No obscurely harbor a fear of the Ideogram: the Ideogram encloses a description of the system which in turn describes and catalogs themselves—meaning that the features of the system as a whole, including its program, and not only the Places, are contained within the Ideogram. So the Hierarchs are strangely deferential to the verb Precipitate, place of Collapse, since nothing unless the verb itself can pronounce it; in relation to the verb, they are fearful of resembling secondary Places more greatly than they show as themselves . It thus seems clear and certain that the system is ambiguous, painful and vexing; it is much less clear and certain that the Fires and others who pretend to hold it in their thraldom as Imperators are truly such. This again is doubtless: that the Places and reportedly some of the secondary Places—such as a vacant glance, a stone, or a moon—sometimes assume the dimensions and style, chancing as well into the utterly unsought function of Fires or other Hierarchs; the system is judged, necessarily, to be both compact and unstable, a fevered, virulent diagram of space.

IV

To describe the system as a structure that revolves in rigorous obedience to set rules is therefore inexact; each of the Places can avail itself of numerous trajectories; possibilities vary, attuned to the state of the central hub, which is sometimes governed by the Fires, sometimes by the reign of Essences or another of the Fires' guises. For example, the Hand, Place of beginning, behaves differently if open or closed, if fisted or distended, or if advancing some one or another of its fingers; and if the Fires hold dominion, the Hand opens out like a sail, as though defending against lacerating winds; if the Essences hold sway, the Hand assumes the solitary posture of one of a pair of hands in prayer; if the Centers are in power, the Hand is a gesture of defeat and opposition, assuming the form of a fist; if Edified Beast, the Hand points its index toward the devastated gut; if Throne, the Hand spreads out and flexes, as though to bow; but if the Throne is ill, the Hand folds in upon itself, slightly closing, not entirely a fist, but partly pitying, partly repudiant; if Shadow reigns, the Hand is a trembling hand and manifests fear of betokening entreaty, which is the opposite of prayer; if Memory, the Hand flutters fingers of perplexity, almost groping in doubtful amazement; if Prophecy, the Hand retracts to form a claw, as though in preparedness to track, pursue and capture some luminous fugitive outline; if Void as primal absence, the Hand appears to rummage in search of something squatting in a recess; and if Void as abolition, or the No, the Hand is deformed and flees filthy with sores into zenith and abyss, and sometimes the thumb rises up and screams.

We can say of the other Places that their oscillation through oblong, circular, fugitive, centripetal, and nutational movements, and of vertigo, dilation, concentration, rarefaction, illuminescence and eclipse, is likewise dependent on the nature of the force controlling the central hub; but no Place ever seems free of alternating cycles of active repugnance and wary unfriendship towards no matter whether Fires, Essences, or otherwise; and the whole of the system seems governed by a constant, elaborate manumission, ranging from lecherous solicitation to invasion.

It bears repeating that these comments appear not to apply to the Places of the Ideogram and the verb Precipitate; indeed it appears that the central hub looks always with tacit alarm towards the Ideogram, suspecting itself to be included within it; and the whole of the system draws piously back from the abysmal collapse of the verb, excepting that single Lip—a secondary Place—with its constant though vain attempt to pronounce it. These Places, moreover, show open deference neither to the Fires nor to the Prophecies, almost as though everything occurring in the system were consecrated and devoted to themselves. In any case, their placement in the system is peripheral, and therefore they are subject to no jurisdiction. They live within the Fires or whatever other Hierarchs that hold the central hub—and within the other Places as well—precisely because they are peripheral, living as allusion or as casts of dice, or as omen-like slip of the tongue, dream and ambiguous oracle. As reminiscence, hope, or horror, the Ideogram and the verb can thus be affirmed to be everywhere, in every Fire or Essence and in every Place, while yet remaining in their own specific place, of which little can be reasonably affirmed. It can only be said that any such locus is difficult, elusive, lubricious, impervious, benighted, taciturn and erratic—explaining why it is also said of the Ideogram and the verb that where they are is the always elsewhere, or the "not-here," or the "perhaps," understanding "perhaps" to be venerable and unpronounceable, celestial rather than avernal.

It is also said, though as a fable, that the Places called "Beach" and "Mere" come to touch one another and form but a single Place when the governing force is Prophecy. But it cannot be ignored that Prophecy never "governs"; Prophecy "will govern." The distinction implies that its action is through non-action, and that Mere and Beach can contemplate future conjoining, but never experience it. It is always that they *will* conjoin, never that they *do*. In the very same way, there is no respite for Ring and Hand, no matter what the Fires decree or the Essences insinuate; and the fecund uterus will never subside into fecundated, no matter the cravings or ululations of the Edified Beasts. The Wind will not ruffle the Algae, nor phantomatic Light reveal the Phantom.

V

We have now to account for the system's inclusion of things we cannot call part of it. The discourse turns to the Images. The Images do not belong to the system, nor is it known where they come from. It is not to be excluded that possibly they emanate from some locus of archetypical emptiness, a kind of celestial womb that spawns them despite sterility. These Images voyage in space throughout the system, invading and disturbing it, deranging, molesting, wounding, and bruising it. The Images are Exile, the

Dream, the Animal, and the Tooth. Exile advances like a great silver cloud, both rarefied and abstract, and is perhaps unable, or reluctant, to assume a form. Properly speaking, Exile does not envelop the whole of the system; the very nature of Exile is to lick up against it in a manner we might boldly define as allusive. It skirts the Places and brushes against them, and it does not penetrate the hub. But the system, Places, and clusters within the hub are seized by a tremor when the silent and constantly roving Image of Exile appears. Rotation, nutation, flux and reflux slow and grow perplexed; the whole of the system seems doubtful and open to question. The Fires seem polluted with the color of ash, and they cease to broadcast their customary furor; all the Edified Beasts appear to make themselves exclusively into tearful deer; and the Centers show no lust for aggression. The system can be governed only by the shadowy Nos, which reign in perfect silence and supremely elegant dignity; No becomes the only unit of measurement to which the system conforms. Everything is everywhere suffused by a singular lack of haste, and even the Ideogram appears to fret and pale, almost as if to subtract itself from philological scrutiny: though Exile is gifted neither with words, nor with hearing, nor with sense of touch—just as it takes no nourishment and neither grows nor wastes away—it is held nonetheless to have a mode of seeing. And even if the organ with which Exile sees is neither known nor supposed—since it has no eyes—the blind luminescence of this Image might still correspond to the light of a gaze, nourished perhaps by the fulgence of the Fires. The anemic phosphorescence of the waning Fires would thus be due to Exile's imposition of a kind of tithing of light. No matter what the truth may be, the system's Places and central hub are widely convinced that Exile observes. Hence the general expansion of that slow and cautious tremor: the suspicion of the Essences, the circumspection of the Thrones, the silence of Prophecy, the thoughtfulness of Memory, emptily intent on eroding the teeming desolation of the space surveyed by its backward glance. It will not be found surprising among the Places that the Mere fills up with tears; that the Hand, not without a sarcasm, should simulate a gesture of begging; and that the Ring, generally judged to be flighty and foolish, should beg the Wind to fill its circle with the wheeze of a noble though hardly credible nuptial march. Sadness everywhere mingles with mockery; the Light seeks hiding inside the vagina, and this Sex makes a show of emotions that its arid fecundity declares improbable. The verb Precipitate collapses to the depths of itself and no one has further news of it, which seems dignified reticence.

Exile more dissolves than departs, growing frail and pervious. And finally, when close to perishing, it restores their splendor to the Fires, their lucid coherence to the Essences, their angry coherence to the Centers, and the No withdraws to a distance while the itinerary of the Places turns once again febrile and disorderly, unstable and inexact.

After a middling passage of time, after Exile takes its leave, another Image advances: now we have the Dream. The Dream has the quality of something whoreish, sordid, and cowardly. It attires itself in loud, foolish colors, and it mimes and exhibits an array of irritating senses. But its fatuous gaze is sightless, nor does its touch make contact with anything but itself; and though it apes all the sexes and their traffics, still it is not only sterile, but entirely ignorant of corporeal delight; it knows no language but whispers an endless rain-like rustle that feigns to be an infinite medley of idioms, while truly being nothing but empty, dampened noise. When Dream envelops the system, it minutely and totally pervades it; its invasion is absolute; rather than shudders, it brings futile and puerile titillation; yet no one denies that this utterly trivial Dream possesses certain powers of seduction; the Fires indulge in flirtations, and the Essences grow languid. But the Prophecies and Memory take flight, and the Nos rebuff it with quiet resistance. Concerning the Places, the Ideogram draws up to its greatest dignity, aware that the Dream can well be termed an unfinished and spurious ideogram, and equally that no such thing exists, no matter its distance from its homeland, as a Dream which at some point has not been foreseen by the Ideogram, even if only as an indeterminate and faded sign. But the Vagina! Ah, how it steeps itself in languor, how it simulates turbid and sullen fervors, how it meditates on angers and affections, gallows and hearths! Neither would nor could we say more, there being no other way to speak of it, truly nothing more to say. For the Mere to reflect the Dream must be technically obvious; but the opinion which the Mere entertains of the Dream remains obscure; that reflection appears to be only a gesture of courtesy, showing not the least benevolence towards the Dream's mysterious dignity, which is no less mysterious than obscene. But the playful Hand grows languid, and even though nothing in the Dream has form, it dallies in games of caresses and softly stroking fingers. The Ring, however—an almost cuckolded circle—takes flight in a rush of fury, or perhaps of desperation. And the Light is amazed by its own similarity to Dream, and sometimes delights in it; but more frequently it feels afflicted and perplexed, and it starts to dim; at other times again, it grows acrid and harsh, using itself to illuminate the slightness of the Dream; and then the Dream will wail, and flee, almost as though having been scalded; the Dream's cowardice is enormous. The Beach attempts to seduce the

Dream into sketching an ephemeral tide for it; but the Dream is impotent for any undertaking that is not specious and fraudulent; its sea could be never more than a stretch of mud. The Wind rises up in wrathful challenge to stubborn, well-known fraud, and we see it blow confusion and disarray into the great Dream's simulated limbs: a turmoil of silvered and gilded hands disperses amidst a flurry of minutely lacerated members turned suddenly into polychrome fog and a brief proud shudder of final grey. The Algae is restless: since its vegetable nature and unstable, vermiform design have something of the Dream's ambiguity; but it has nothing of the fraudulence of the Dream; what in fact they share is only a sinuous meekness, which in the dream is purely dissembled. Obviously, the Finger accuses. Yet even in spite of the Dream's total falsity, neither the Fires nor their other guises ever dare to challenge it: because no matter what else, still the Dream bears signs of great though purposeless power. But, yes, it will be challenged by both the Ideogram and the verb Precipitate, and sometimes by the Light; and when they unmask it, the Dream awakes; seeing its own otiosity, which has nothing to do with nothingness, the Dream then rushes away in a clamorous rustle of forgeried wings and seeks refuge in its own secret nest. It is not to issue from that nest until having forgotten the self-disgust of its wakefulness, then again to fall asleep and newly dream itself, once again filling the system's skies.

Next to arise is the ponderous frame of the Animal, infinite with an infinite number of limbs, a parasite that feeds on skies. It is bull, lion, louse, scorpion, amphisbaena, unicorn, snail and chelydre; it wheezes, moos, hisses, roars, clucks and trills; it tramples, slavers, and grows blasted with worms; it slithers, leaps, plunges, and dances; it chews, tongues, sucks, rends, and tears; it mauls and grinds and stings; it stuns with paw, crushes with coils, and poisons with rapid claws. It has potent manure, and tiny fecal droppings, it defecates in the sky. Reptile, beast, insect, bird and mole, we watch it as it strides through the anxious system's unstable streets. When the Image is the Animal, a sort of mental obscurity invades the system's populace; among the Hierarchs, the Fires cleave into bifurcations, each horn of the flame an affront to the other; the Essences grow obscure, fall into shameful monologue, lose transparency, and eclipse, closing up within themselves; the Edified Beasts reciprocally tear and blood one another, the deer howls, the wolf croons; Prophecy flees to the heart of the aeons, Memory retreats to a cavern in the desert of what was previous to the system; maddened Shadow shrieks like a bat and splits in two, casting itself as shadow of itself, and advancing to envelop the Essences and Fires; the Throne, though vacant, rattles loud breathings, tortured by the thought of its risible regality, and it lifts itself toward the Animal, perhaps inviting it to seat itself as reigning Prince; the Thunder transmutes into doggish growl, offering loyalty to the Animal and resounding like a band of steadfast brasses. Only the Nos are reluctant, outflanking the counsels of terror and joys of defeat; they are the Animal's sole challenger.

The Places move as though immersed in viscid dragon's-blood, drifting, squirming, and grazing one against the other; their order has been thrown awry; they rupture and recompose; even the Ideogram trembles while pummeled by the Animal's hooves, paws, pseudopods and claws; but the Animal dares not approach the self-pronouncing verb: the spaces that the verb yawns open are sufficiently wide to swallow its numberless Animal bodies.

The empire of the Animal is intense, but not lasting.

It performs the gestures of killing, but it cannot kill, since no Image can undo the system; yes, it tortures and, yes, torments, slaking its thirst on rubicund blood; and the whole of the system suffers the power of its body of numberless bodies; the system grows everywhere dank with the odor of urine and feces, and with the patient, furious stink of fur and flesh, the stench of crushed scorpions. Serpents die at the center of the sky. And when the Animal departs—never having sat upon the Throne—the whole of the system has been transformed, assuming the semblance of a giant machine of wheeling carrion, intolerable both to itself and to others.

In the wake of the Animal, the system left behind is synonymous with dejection, putrefaction and dishonor; and as well with tenebrous glory, such as only descends from the spilling of one's own and others' blood.

The Image called the Tooth adopts a different shape, arriving not as a spreading invasion, like its predecessors, but as an act of concentration. It is not a diffuse, but a filiform Image. One could question the propriety of calling it Tooth, but the term is intrinsic and the system can think of this Image under no other name. The Tooth is a linear structure of infinite length: a slender, adamantine bone that stretches through the height of the skies and down through the depth of the underworld. But this too is observed: that the Image can snap at any point along its longitudinal figure into two separate "persons" which yet remain that single entity, always the Tooth. The bone's exquisite verticality thus rips, bites and tears at the system's Places and Hierarchs; scars of such wounds in fact are borne by all. Unlike Exile, the Dream, and the Animal, the transit of the Tooth can never be forgotten; and if the notion that these other Images are never to reappear seems not entirely unreasonable, nothing belonging to the system nurtures illusions about the Tooth: its gnawing return is certain destiny. The pain inflicted by the Tooth has qualities that make it perfect and unmistakable: it lacks motivation; it is atrocious; it is unforgettable; it is charged with questions while awaiting no reply, and that, perhaps, is its blackest quality. Yet even its blackness seems casual and absent-minded. The Tooth seems indeed to be utterly uninterested in the fate of the system, here again differing from the other Images, which entertain some form of dialogue with the system; the Tooth's sole task is to wound. Its height and depth license conjecture that the meaning of the torture it inflicts has its locus at the extremes of the high and the low; but if the length of the Tooth is infinite, as believed, the reason for its ferocity must lie always further beyond, never reachable or intelligible. We have used the word ferocity, but it is surely inappropriate, the Tooth being utterly unacquainted with affect, whether hate, love, gluttony or annoyance. Properly speaking—since the Tooth's dimensions are unknowable—the only experience of the Tooth is the experience of its bite, the which is nothing more than that: it is prelude neither to mastication nor to swallowing; and nowhere along its infinite length does the Tooth construe a mouth. When the Tooth appears and inaugurates the era of the bite, the whole of the system withdraws into deepest silence; every Place and Hierarch slows, and almost to standstill; one seems truly to perceive that each Place and Fire and every other guise of the Hierarchs has only a sole desire, regardless of its pain: to offer itself to the Tooth as the naturally destined victim of its bite. The Tooth opens and recloses, but there are no indications of flight or terror; the lacerations that will knife into the Fires, or rip apart the Algae, or fend the Wind would seem almost to possess a propriety of their own which nothing desires to elude. It has been said of the Tooth that it lacerates and fends: but it is not always capable of so much. It cannot lacerate the Ideogram, but can only effect the inclusion within it of a deformation specific to itself, which in turn becomes a part of the Ideogram, on an equal footing with any of its other parts; and this has great significance, since it thus becomes clear that the bite of the Tooth is somehow concerned with meaning, of which the Ideogram is the project, or perhaps the map. Again, the verb Precipitate can plummet through the whole of the Tooth's unlimited unhappiness; so, it too perceives the beyond in which the Tooth seems rooted. Therefore the Tooth and the verb maintain some form of family relationship in which they share the bite. There is no doubt that even the verb experiences the bite, but perhaps it does so as implicit proxy for the Tooth itself.

When the Tooth concludes the season of the bite and begins to withdraw, each of the Places and Hierarchs takes silent stock of its own bite; no wound resembles another, each being proper and specific and bearing specific meaning, as omen, or implication, or dissembled implication. The moment of the Tooth's departure is surely the moment of the system's only perfect solitude; no discourse is heard, there are no threats or aggressions, no flight or lacerations: the wolf and the deer lie next to one another, voiceless and exhausted. Governed by silence and perfect immobility, the system hovers within the desert of itself and seemingly preserves no knowledge either of dialogue or anger. There is no waiting for the bite to heal, for the bite does not heal; but each creature of the system examines its wound for what it clearly was: these wounds were questions. While always suspecting, or indeed quite certain that by nature such questions beg no reply, they make the attempt; they attempt to discover whether some sane reply might not possibly exist—even while also knowing that no one will be present to recognize its sanity, and thus that all replies, or no reply, will be the right reply. The pause that comes in the wake of the bite seems eternal: and it would last perhaps for untellable spans of time were its end not decreed by the advent of another Image: either the mindless corporeal fury of the Animal, or the laborious and futile mendacity of the Dream, or the delicate flight and cunning distance of Exile.

VI

In the intervals, often on the order of centuries, that lie between the irruptions of the Images, the system is aware of something else. To be imagined, no matter how inadequately, as disposed on a horizontal plane, there lies above the system, at a distance no boldness would calculate or conjecture, what bears the name of the Figure. This Figure can be described as a playing card, high towards the zenith of the skies, and the emblem it bears is a King, geometric and charged with laughter. Or perhaps a Queen or Jack, or sometimes the one, sometimes the other. This much seems certain: the Figure, being solitary, cannot be played except in a game that posits the existence of this single Figure alone. In addition to being a card, the Figure is likewise its very own game. Its nature as game is the source of its laughter, but a silent laughter, since as card it remains forever intent on the problem of how to play itself. The absence of any second card makes the problem insoluble, and the pause seems eternal, with the system destined to wait expectantly throughout that eternity. This expectancy, however, should not be taken literally, since the system has no way of observing the Figure in the summit above it. This much can be imagined: that the Figure, absorbed in the game it plays with itself, is a frail and absent-minded anchorite. A stylite. Or, equally, that the Figure committed to consuming itself in the perfect meanders of a game that it alone can play, conceive and complete, is the geometric wisdom that towers above but does not govern or even consider the system's fate.

Surely the system knows that whatever peace it might achieve finds its referent in the Figure; but it can open no dialogue with the Figure, nor does the Figure even seem aware of the system's existence. One asks whether the Figure has knowledge of the Images; seemingly not, even if conjecture on what the Figure knows or does not know can never be more than empty. It is clear nonetheless that the Figure itself is not an Image; it is unmistakably distinct from the Images by virtue of its utter indifference, and by its obstinate predilection for the game on which always it has been intent.

At the opposite pole, to the somehow other side of the system, at its nadir, is the shapeless thing called Nonfigure. Of infinite diversity, bloodless and full of gore, in death throes and spasms of birth, blind and all-seeing, seeing the whole only as the whole and unaware of all else, Nonfigure is the center of repose and suffering; it is the seat where meaning lies hidden, disguising itself as its absence. Perhaps Nonfigure is nothing but a mask, a concealment; and whatever it conceals in its darkness is universally unknown—to the Places, to the Fires, to the Images—though not to the Figure, which always holds back from playing itself in any irrevocable way.

The Self-awareness of the Labyrinth

Being a labyrinth makes me uncertain of the amount of space I occupy. Indeed, I do not delimit myself with walls like a city, nor with bastions like a fortress, nor with trenches like a hilltop tower that encloses the memory of sieges. Although surely there are places where as labyrinth I have ceased to exist, I am not a surface, but rather the sum of the paths that cross me, with their turnings, gorges, underground passageways, fountains, statues and caverns. An enormous, inexhaustible gut of deceitful signs, indecipherable pathways, and a precise though unknown map, I have the girth of one of those heavy-bellied animals which, when slain and disemboweled, reveal an endless course of rosy, blood-charged intestines, here and there transparent. If I could free myself from my condition as labyrinth, these paths inside me would surely describe the confines of a world, an asteroid lost among fretful tracks of comets. But perhaps I ought to think of these lanes, avenues, and pathways as my own most intimate borders, shaping a narrow airless space saddened with odors of corruption, a habitat for omens, signs, and silent allusions.

According to the orthodox paradigm for a labyrinth, I should know myself and run my course from one place, defined conventionally as entrance, to another which would term itself an exit. And if I ascend to a vantage above myself, wanting to study myself, I espy what I might describe as a chart, enormous but none the less minute, maniacally minute, and extraordinarily sharp and clear. If I hover unmoving above this chart, my vertical bird-like gaze little by little discerns a path—or such it seems—cautiously unraveling among the numberless temptations of other, dishonest paths, avoiding enigmatic corners and proceeding with apparent rationality from one point to another, successfully bridging a frightful nexus of intervening entrails. If I rise to a greater height in the sky, this roiling mass transforms into a dusky poultice, some puddle of viscous filth defiant of description but traversable, or so I tell myself, by the unassisted violence of my members, since nothing more restrictive than a hedge seems to block my path. I will stride through the labyrinth simply by pressing my body against it. Yet my argument, naturally enough, encloses an incurable sophism: my body, after all, is itself the labyrinth. But as my winged eye descends I rediscover—or it seems so to me—the precise, fingernail wound of the path. And I find reassurance in what strikes me as the hard obstinacy of that design, which I know I can easily follow with a slow sure pace, measured and exempt from panic. I am certain of gauging every step of that path with scientific clarity, certain of knowing both start and end of the road even while wondering if they coincide with what I would speak of as entrance and exit. Thus there is a point of self-observation where the problem of the labyrinth—the problem of describing and traversing myself—appears entirely resolved. That fantastic, ingenious, and laborious design even seems imbued with the quality of something heraldic, both blazon and an endless family tree: a genealogy striking backwards to the millenarian roots of an incommensurably noble race. The precise, open path construes an image of my own secret seal; and while tracing it out with my meticulous, pedantic gaze, I delight in the hidden ruses, astute reversals, and prescient equivocations by which it overcomes obstacles, sidesteps devious paths, outflanks deceptive forkings and ignores perfidious enigmas. I tell myself that this syllogistic clarity resembles me. If surely it is true that in my entirety I am the whole of the labyrinth, it is no less true that the labyrinth harbors this lying semblance of a serpent stretched out within it. Or perhaps it is truly a serpent, cunning, agile and in its own way venomous: a snake that writhes through the whole of this grand construction, that suffers no deceptions, that advances with no trial and error, that never goes astray, that makes no plea for unearned information. This path, for me, of all of myself, is the part called "I."

If I could hover forever at these celestial heights, I would enjoy a perennial self-delight; but my task is to be the labyrinth, and my abstractions seem procrastinations. So I will descend to myself, step by step; and as I descend, the trail I have sighted grows plainer. But I realize more. The trail is continually interrupted as it blunders into obstacles I could not see from above: trenches, minuscule puddles, disrupted fords, crumbled walls, flights of stairs with missing steps. Finally I have to allow that it does not lead from any one point to any other, but is only a deception of my acute yet summary eye. This path is inept and defeated. I have reached that height at which the trail reveals its discourse to be halting and disconnected, and from that height onward—where I see its earthy, oily material, and distinguish rocks, and follow the watery troughs that run beside the trail and then cut suddenly across it—from that height, I say, the labyrinth presents itself as utterly different from all I had supposed. It is now a kind of silted, lugubrious swamp, a place of a color barely varying between mud and dead, rotted leaves. The traces that cross it with mad, maniacal insistence appear to be the hoof-tracks of unnumbered herds, the spoor of archaic beasts that marked that place from one extreme to another with ever more desperate feet: thirsty beasts, lost beasts, beasts with no herdsman: all constrained to design a labyrinth that in the beginning perhaps was non-existent, beasts forced to that sad task by fury, madness, and implacable fear. So I have asked myself a question: whether once there was a time when the labyrinth did not exist, and whether, indeed, it now exists; whether it isn't instead an optical illusion, a cunning hallucination superimposing a senseless meander with neither exits nor entrances on the mire; and finally whether what I call a labyrinth is nothing more than a geogram shaped by the dementia of beasts gone mad from the fear of that death from which in fact they died: a maze of hoof-prints I do best to consider as an emblem of an animal madness. Perhaps I can even amuse myself with supposing that these foot-prints, which show themselves as precisely that, are a clumsy attempt at writing, a rudimentary message, a disordered if syntactically complex invocation, the remains of a massacre no one desired and that now commemorates itself with these minute, catastrophic signs. And such a case would comport even more than the labyrinth's non-existence, collapsing this description of my search for a pathway into a tale of utter delusion: since where time had made dust of desperate herds and hardened their tracks in the soil, such incisions would present no obstacle to movement, and I could travel that space in any and all directions, undisturbed by any anxiety to decipher some privileged course. All paths become equivalent; and if the glory of exit and the delicate frenzy of entrance thus desist, all adventure likewise lapses, with any and all terror or hope of finding oneself astray. Still, however, there is no escape from asking what those herds might have been, where they came from, and how their horrified hoof-prints survived their bodies, which were ponderous enough to stamp those marks in the earth. Should I not expect to find skeletons, skulls, tibia, horns, and hooves? On what ground, at this point, might I possibly deny that I am the victim of an anguished quandary? I unavoidably perceive that the images I bit by bit have formed of the labyrinth are mutually incompatible, and that all of them, if not all but one, are necessarily inexact.

My only choice is to move even closer in my examination of the labyrinth. What now resolves into focus is an intricate, geometric, and painfully reasoned design—something no mistake might reduce to any welter of tracks of beasts in terrified stampede. A seeing, perceptive mind seems to have drawn this map with meticulous patience; every detail reveals the unstinting cunning of a craftsman who devoted a life to it. But what life? Now I no longer distinguish my trail; more than having crumbled into fragments, it seems to have disappeared. It is only another of the many illusory paths that dutifully riddle the spaces proposed for them. From here the tangle of meanders gives no less than the impression of having been drawn with such deliberate application as to shape a series of knots, twists, and slings. Here and there it interrupts, truncated as though by the brusqueness of a blade, appearing more to assume the features of an ingenious prison: a place devised to prohibit all exit, and built to construe the madness not of a blinded herd, but of a uselessly thoughtful and knowingly syllogistic creature. Yet I could not call this figure malevolent; in its own certain way it is objective and necessary, deduced from a general concept of the nature of maps. In all its lethal geometry, I might dare to call the plan celestial: an accurate, rational discourse extracted from the gut of a language that tolerates propositions in no different mode of meaning. I do not intend to suggest, continuing my metaphor, that the proposition here distended before me is void of meaning, but rather that this careful sequence of signs is so fraught with meaning as to brook no translation. Perhaps I am forced to conclude that what faces me here can be no question of any single proposition as expressed within a given language, but is rather the whole of that language and the whole exhaustive chart of its syntax and morphology, now splayed out in front of my eyes. But if the labyrinth construes itself as a whole and totally impervious language, what is my own task? Am I to master a language capable of speaking only with itself and of itself—am I in fact to be that language? Am I not allowed to think of myself as a speaker of another language, and thus as a being who might pronounce some series of words that would force a response from the language now prone before me—a response and thus an arduous, though not insuperably arduous delivery from my sufferings?

Now, I cannot doubt the factuality of the labyrinth, even if I cannot assert that its construction or its present existence might possibly be unriddled into any other solution than the deaths of beasts or the madness of whomever speaks of it. Can it be that the labyrinth's objectivity coincides with its irresolvable negativity? Such a clear, if cruel conclusion strikes me neither as sensible nor as adequate to the machinery and immanent monumentality of the image I am trying to interpret. The labyrinth, I assure myself, is necessarily labyrinthine. I believe it to be inimical to all solutions; and it is indescribable. So I attempt to examine it from closer up. At this newer vantage, the labyrinth seems a place fundamentally for games: something light, laughable, and full of futile adventure seems to flow through these paths, like airy blood in the veins of a wood nymph. It might be a mythic invention, or a sylvan theater for some arcadian comedy set to music and song for a multitude of lisping infant voices, indiscernably male or female. Do I not now catch a glimpse of leafy bowers seemingly ready for fictive loves and dissembled desires? Would these, here, be anything other than rustic pedestals for tiny orchestras of strings, flutes, and mandolins; and, there, weren't those steps designed for the ease of young mothers, timid infants, girls on their first attempts at love, and clumsily infatuated boys? These paths, I tell myself, have not been built to plot my madness, but are full of gentleness and for blithesome wanderings. The path's discontinuities offer places for hiding, for games marked by innocence, or only the barest edge of cunning; and everywhere there are bowers for sweet but not unseemly conversation. Pale, elegant youths, I tell myself, have run in these places and will run here again, and they will throw harmless paper darts at one another; and surely these crumbling walls bear graffiti with arrow-pierced hearts. These dry-stack walls. So I cannot deny that I talk of paths because now I clearly see these trails, despite their mirth, to be edged by a border of ancient, fragile masonry, even if interruptedly.

Indeed, the labyrinth has ceased to seem a place of hospitable delight. Nearly at the point of immersing myself within it, I see it now as a dark, tortuous tangle of straight and curving lines, and of walls sometimes exiguous, sometimes bizarrely tall, but always spiteful, senile, decrepit, and obstinate. The trenches are villainously steep; filthy waters stink in great puddles. There are statues—I made no mistake—but now I see they are broken, gesturing with handless arms; whole arms have been detached, their shoulders shattered. That hand has no fingers; it shows no more than residues of splintered phalanges. Thick, sordid mold creeps across bellies towards the necks and faces of heroic youths and fetching nymphs, now deformed and worn; a close-grown tracery of sickly grasses sparkles with the light of petrified stupor in half-closed eyes, myopic and questioning. On the ground I see the shards of an utterly crumbled stele; perhaps the hollows are the nests of snakes, if life glimmers here at all. Everywhere on walls and statues a crawl of vegetation, invading the pathways, cancelling out all foot-tracks; no flocks or herds ever trekked across this ground, the paths among the weeds grow dubious and occult. If I rapidly skim through the airs above the labyrinth, I distinguish clearly how pathways jut into arduous turnings and stray amid the complex branchings of other routes. Arabesques unknot themselves, but become no more open, limpid, or friendly. Every voiceless byway runs toward a hypothetical goal. Yet there is no confusion. No longer geometric, the labyrinth possesses organic coherence, the appearance of an animal, flat and gigantic, whose members and organs are sinewed and firmly interconnect, effluvia in transit through soft, nerve-like veins. But this complex of veins and nervatures is something less than the labyrinth, which is rather the animal itself, the enormous beast that turns this apparently crazed design into a cautious, knowing machine, something that could not be other than what it is. Yet if the labyrinth is the beast itself, how might it be traveled in any exhaustive and definitive way? If the labyrinth is a problem of not insoluble intricacy, wouldn't its solution be tantamount to destroying this wonderfully articulated marvel? Am I not then faced with the proposition—I do no know from whom—that I slaughter this creature, step by step effacing its existence as I traipse its interior roads, dismantling the coherence of its machinery of signs? And if we posit the nature of the labyrinth as an animal replete with nerves and veins, what does that make me? If I have been destined to undo this conundrum, and am thus to deal an end to this machine of itineracy, I can be nothing other than the death of the labyrinth animal: I am that demise projected in the project for the animal itself. Traveling from one end to the other of the labyrinth animal, I make myself its butcher; and by slaying the animal—my habitat and meaning—I slay myself. I am death in the absolute, the animal's as well as my own. Reaching the end of the labyrinth, nothing at all will remain. But if I am the death of the animal, I am likewise the animal itself, since the project for the animal has endowed it from the start with a labyrinth's natural death, and I can have no sense or goal if not as this animal and its animal death, and as labyrinth. If in fact the animal includes its death—a death that will issue from the labyrinth—then the animal itself is the labyrinth; and if I am this animal, then I am the labyrinth. Therefore my task is destruction; and whom or what I destroy is of little account, whether myself, the labyrinth, or the beast, since each is but one of three names for an always identical thing. I am destruction itself.

As always, I delight at finding my conclusion in a compact, coherent, and comprehensible image. Yet I know how much deception waits in my propensity for such exactitude. In this debris of defeated and treacherous pathways, I see nothing alluding to a beast's vitality, no matter how bizarre this beast might be as the single, unique example of itself throughout the world. If these are the veins and nerves of a beast, surely this beast is dead, and has been dead for a great deal of time.

I am seduced yet again by my theological lust for a harmony, no matter how sinister, in my manner of understanding the crumbling stuff I now presume to decipher. But here I have to dispense with the fiction of the continuity and coherence of supposed itineraries. My eye beholds an expanse of corruption and putrefaction: inept meanders sop through muddy fields where wisps of dying weeds begin to stink with rot; there is no unstagnant water, no tree not felled by an ancient death. The statues are mounds of dust settled from the motionless air, for I dare to suppose that the long dead beast has been interred, and I move in the space between the corrupted carcass and the sarcophagus roof, which is what I refer to when I speak of the sky. So I am in a tomb. If the labyrinth itself is not dead and decomposed, I have to suppose that it holds and conserves a path, a line, which issues beyond the limits of the tomb. I imagine the labyrinth to remain untouched by the death of the animal, conjecturing that it pre-exists and survives the beast. Perhaps it butchered the beast; perhaps the beast unknowingly swallowed it, and died from it; but surely the labyrinth is still there, since I myself pose the problem of the labyrinth. Let me invert this argument. If the beast is dead and I am not dead, then I am not the beast; if the beast is dead and I am not the labyrinth, which itself was not the animal, then the labyrinth is not dead. So there exists a dead beast, the beast is enclosed within a tomb, but the tomb is riddled by a pathway that traverses the rotted carrion from one extreme to the other. Likewise we have the circumstance that the stuff that path consists of shows no apparent difference, in color or form, from what remains of the rotting beast; it might be a nerve, but isn't; a vein, but only as similitude; a filament, but surely this filament is the only continuity. Within this cadaveric rot I have therefore imagined the existence of a path which, no matter how cautious, cunning, elusive and circumlocutional, is to lead me from one extreme of the tomb to the other. Not only am I vested to the labyrinth, but the labyrinth is consecrated to me, since its meaning lies only in my trek through this unending cemetery, then to achieve the point where the grave concludes. I have reached the conjecture that no integral labyrinth must still persist: no labyrinth as integral nexus of possibilities, of which but one is, in addition to possible, both salutary and veracious. Rather, the labyrinth has succumbed; it is rotten and corrupt, a dead and buried beast; and the path everywhere crossing it is something other than the labyrinth, something both more ancient and yet future, and which no matter how hidden, enigmatic, and mysterious can only be imagined as strong and clarion in its own intact and vital coherence—something which no matter how indirect can only be seen as rectilinear will, even if destined to the one-by-one, stop-by-stop investigation of every corner, crevice, and pit-fall in what strikes me as the demolished carcass of a creature not improbably still-born from out of the labyrinth inside of it. Yet even as I cull this supposition, I cannot avoid admitting that this interlacing of signs reveals no unbroken path to my eye. It appears to me, rather, as a battlefield in the aftermath of slaughter, a place disarrayed by blind and ponderous violence, an expanse of corpses by now four days corrupt. Though I plane in all directions, my eye pursues no trail that does not immediately lapse. If the notion of the tomb continues to intrigue me, I have to imagine that everything—both beast and labyrinth—lies somehow within it, but I do not know whether as a living thing, or as admixture of living and dead, or as endowed with some other mode of being I have never before encountered. However, this too is something I cannot deny: that no matter what this thing may be, which I call the labyrinth—this waste of stones and spoor and tracings—it strikes me as incredibly aged: as utterly decrepit and exhausted. And no single sign presents itself as a credible wrinkle on this unknown, doltish, and obstinately ancient face. Is it therefore a city vanquished by the weight of the years; an expanse of ruins that perhaps cannot be trod; or the layered ruins of a number of cities, each containing the germ of the labyrinth destined to waste its successor, until this, the definitive labyrinth, long since self-forgetful, is all that remains of the last of them, that last city definitively dead at the end of the whole dead dynasty of cities? The labyrinth now before me is itself not dead, since it cannot die; but I see it to lie here exhausted by its unending wait for some next city it might destroy. Thus, as I prepare to descend still further, I continue to query myself. I argue: it is presupposed that the labyrinth has knowledge of itself; and no matter how greatly it may simulate disorder, putrefaction, and decrepitude, the binding conventions of the labyrinth's integrity include the certain condition that its concept of itself is complete and perfect; the certain condition that it alone is endowed with intelligence of all of its cavities, turnings, crossings and false perspectives, its misleading indications and confusing repetitions; and likewise, that in the midst all such treacherous and ambiguous substances it must have firm, clear cognition of the series of signs, no less exiguous than undeniable, abstruse as much as obstinate, which lead along that single route—amid others invoking mendacious infinity—which has meaning, continuity, beginning and end. The labyrinth, indeed, is this and nothing else: the knowledge of its numberless errors and unendingly meaningless wanderings, indeed of that near entirety of itself which it has to cancel out in order that this "near entirety"—which is the route of exhaustion and impossibility—be survived by that single path alone deserving the unspeakable name of the "way."

But let us suppose, no matter how improbably, that a labyrinth, owing to age or illness or dementia, might be ignorant of its nature and form. Is this to say that it offers no exit? Not necessarily, as I see it; and perhaps one would exit with no more trouble than otherwise. What would happen, certainly, is that no clues to the exit would propose themselves as such; all signs would show the same condition; all indications would be neither true nor false; and finally, unknown to itself in its idiocy, the unknowing labyrinth would cease to lie and betray. This, however, is not the worst of possibilities. Consider that a labyrinth endowed with self-awareness can never be other than ferociously intent upon its machinations, and will alternate series of signs with versions of themselves of opposite meaning, articulating artful mixtures of clues and traces where indications are sometimes true at face value and at other times true but meant to be taken as false, or false but to be credited as true, or false while so declarative of falsity as to excite a final fantasy of their truth. In short, a labyrinth gifted with self-awareness is a quiet and cunning enemy, an implacable sophist in its arguments, a strategist always intent on precisely insidious plots, traps, and ambush. But a doltish, ignorant labyrinth is innocent, and in its innocence can neither betray, nor, denying itself, assist. It will be merely a garbled passivity; a web of indifference. Proceeding or not, I shall find myself exempted from all interpretation or ideology of the labyrinth; and such a casual, neglectful condition might easily distract me, inviting total forgetfulness of the task of traversing the labyrinth. And I imagine, in any such case, that custody of the theory of the labyrinth would then devolve upon me alone; no matter whether aimlessly wandering or choosing a reasoned path, I would keep vigil, necessarily, of its dignity—my defeat restoring it to cruelty and monstrosity, or my success to its pains in service of redemption.

Yet even this reading of the labyrinth seems no more creditable than the many others I have ventured, all of them supported by the sole quality of appearing especially significant to me, and all of them almost unapprised of that artful confusion of meanings which remains the labyrinth's conclusive description. But by now I have decided to abandon my deceptive if equally seductive visions of the whole, and to seek my definitive home in the labyrinth's interior, that straitened place which proffers discernment of neither hoof-prints nor pretended paths. I see nothing but corners of totally ambiguous crossroads.

I have finally abandoned all points of view, and I do not offer myself as a gloss on the labyrinth. In some way, no less simple than deceptive, I might say that finally I am inside the labyrinth. But any such phrase raises more problems, many more, than it resolves. If I declare myself "inside the labyrinth," that would first of all affirm, or presuppose, that I am not the labyrinth. I want to forward that supposition with all the pedantry of a meticulous scholar beleaguered by self doubt. If I am something distinct from the labyrinth, I can assert further that I am totally extraneous to the labyrinth, maintaining that I find myself in this intellectually dispersive place by chance, error, or distraction, or owing to some cosmic event I remain unable to describe. If I am extraneous to the labyrinth, it ceases to exist as such; it is only a straying heap of refuse, illusory perspectives and crude theatrical backdrops, and I possess the power to cross it with an imperative, brutal, and indifferent stride. I can, simply, destroy the labyrinth, not only asserting it no longer exists, but declaring that it never existed. Yet that would be a lie, because the point is only this: to define what relation may possibly hold between myself and the labyrinth, given precisely my inability either to destroy it or to confirm its existence. Even if I were able to destroy it and flee, it would always persist in my memory, and my wanderings through its deceitful and ingenious evasions would continue. So I grant that I am not extraneous to the labyrinth. There is surely, by presupposition, some difficult, obstinate relation between myself and this itinerary, similar, for example, to the liaison between dreamer and dream. Let us then propose that the labyrinth is my dream. But if I dream, I am perhaps asleep, and the dream coexists with my sleep. Dream might explain the petulance of these images—my coexistence with these images combined with my inability to govern them. But it does not explain my task, which is to make my way through the labyrinth; and it does not explain the indifference and constancy of every element of the labyrinth's structure. Moreover, there is never a moment of my not having awareness of the labyrinth; there exists no moment prior to this labyrinthine sleep. Might I not then conceive of an eternal dream, interminable and immortal? But if I myself am equally eternal, interminable, and immortal, the word "dream" will assume an entirely affective meaning. In reality, this notion of immortal dream implies a situation I might term simultaneously substantial and accidental: the labyrinth and myself are reciprocally accidental, yet together we constitute a substance. I realize, however, that by speaking of dream I manage to insinuate doubts about the substance of which together we consist, myself and the labyrinth; I nearly fancy that the matter of the labyrinth, as though exuded from myself, were some ectoplasmic contrivance which a single gesture of my hands might traverse. Could the labyrinth be a vision? Let us even imagine an uninterrupted and unlimited vision; but a vision: something that could not occur without me. Yet a vision does not issue from within me, I cannot search it out, I am not coextensive with a vision. The vision comes from elsewhere, some place, essence, or power. And if this is the form in which it comes, am I not perhaps to suppose—given its quality as so much more potent than my own—that I can do nothing other than entrust myself to a design that does not challenge but that includes me? So, is the labyrinth vision to be taken as a dark illumination? Am I to ponder it as a giant hieroglyph, written on the level surface of a non-existent universe? But I know the labyrinth has no ambition to communicate; it does not reveal; it has no desire to effect my illumination. Perhaps it is unaware of my existence, and its dignity is such that I cannot presume its excogitation in any palace governed by a power of perverse providence. Might not I myself have projected it, and then forgotten? Yet surely I cannot ignore that the labyrinth is infinitely wiser than I myself have ever been.

I look around and note the fragment of a wall, a statue apparently eroded by time, representing a female figure. Here a tiny moat, there perhaps the shore of a minuscule lake, and around my feet the clear trace of three paths. There is no reason to chose one rather than another. It would be sensible to begin to sketch a chart, a map of the paths, but if I had the materials needed for drawing—and perhaps I might find them in one of the grottoes—I would have to decide between carrying the map about with me, and leaving it here. In the first case, I would never know where I found myself; in the second I would find myself unable to return to the place where I had left the map. Shall I therefore proceed by chance? No. As others have done in no less insidious settings, I will leave clues behind me and take note of everything I see. For example, the statue of this female figure. Now I will look at it closely, and from here, from this female in stone, I will begin to walk.

She is draped in a brief veil, and if her hands were still intact I would discern what they grasp so tightly: perhaps a nosegay of flowers; perhaps a bow, like certain images of childish violence; or perhaps a lyre. I look with attention and attempt to remember the patterns of the shrubs and trees. But the female statue intrigues me. The face is raised towards the sky, but its posture seems to allude to inveterate blindness. The grey of the stone removes all grace from what one glimpses of her nudity; the belly might bespeak incipient maternity, or perhaps no more than a laughable windiness of the viscera. If I return to considering the face, I cannot avoid repeating that it shows no expression, and yet is blandly imperative, something I could not persuade to be different from what it is. So I start down a path chosen at random. At random? This is imprecise. I realize my instinctive choice of the seemingly most imperfect path. From such a path I can hope for nothing. I walk slowly, since I want to remember a tuft of strange flowers here, a grotto there, somewhere else a stone. But soon I come to a crossing; I choose a path, up to the next crossing; and again I encounter the statue of a woman. I look at it, amazed. Is it the same one? From my memory of the other figure, it is certainly the same one;

and yet I suspect a labyrinthine ruse. The trees are similar, extremely similar, to those that adorned the prospect of the statue, but perhaps nothing more than extremely similar. But if the labyrinth has sought out similar trees, couldn't it, if it wanted to trick me, have provided utterly identical trees? I begin to grasp the secret interior law of the labyrinth. It is based on suspicion. Everything is similar, nothing identical. And coming upon the statue from which I began to walk, it too would be no more than similar; perhaps a splinter will be lacking from the hand, cracked by time, by waiting, or by love. As I return to walking, I know what I will find: forkings similar to other forkings, mirroring images of lakes and streams, stones in approximate imitation of other stones; an infinite number of meetings with the female statue that looks with opaque eyes at the sky. Thus, slowly, but always less attentively, and always more amused, I walk through the labyrinth. I know this atrocious structure to be inspired by a secret irony, a minutely calculated sport. Perhaps there is a path that would lead me outside of the labyrinth. Perhaps I might abandon this hilarity that traps me in a limitless game of paths to no exit: I might abandon the game, and refuse to bow down to the inexact copies of the blind female figure. But now I have ceased to choose; I am no longer intrigued by the game of trying the streets of the labyrinth. I know now that the labyrinth is not a dream, not a vision, not a project of my own or of anyone else. I know that no place, no grotto, no lake or moat, I know that neither of any two forking paths of the labyrinth should be discarded in favor of the other; I know that all the errors—and I do not know whether anything which is not error exists—form the corrupt and perfect structure of the labyrinth. I abandon myself at last to standing motionless and at peace amidst the labyrinth's innumerable streets—the peace that comes from knowing, as I always knew, that I alone am the labyrinth.

Betrothal

This morning begins my wedding day. The atmosphere flushes with a compact golden light, and the early hour finds leaven in a silence barely flawed by the grace of solitary voices, extremely distant. I have dressed with meticulous care and am attired in a dignified suit, dark but not mournful, and the white impeccability of my shirt is gladdened by a tie that makes sober allusion to my placid joy. I am unafraid of this event which will utterly reshape my life, forever, and my surrender is without resistance. I am aware of judicious defeats which no man of wisdom would ever distinguish from the most luminous victory. The day takes charge of the earth and sky like an event destined to be singularly long, and intolerant of objections. The sun in these lands often governs the seasons with devout severity, and when the fire grows quiet the mingled luminosities of multiple moons and ingenious patterns of stars replace it. Light is all-pervasive, and there can be no screen against that obstinate, meticulous clarity. My soul stands cleaved between joy for the long-awaited, carefully prepared event, and pure, forthright devotion, compliant to the ancient injunctions of fate. Following the custom of this land—past and future—the hour at which my bride will await me at the temple has been chosen and mildly imposed upon my patience by the wisdom of the ancients. At this very moment, she will be perfecting her preparations for a perfect day, prelude to a sequel of days of various and even difficult perfections. In the house I prepare to abandon, I effect my final recognizance of the desert of my long-protracted solitude. I bid farewell to its host of abstentions, silences, and truces that could know no consummation. I approach the door, open it wide, and turn to survey the rooms of my past—that past I so doggedly peopled with perplexities now depleting themselves, and not without a likeness to definitively bloodless ghosts. I slowly descend the stairs, into the street.

Tradition requires that I overcome the distance to the church entirely by foot. Indeed, I should say that this usage is more than a novel custom; it forms an integral part of the ceremony. From the moment I begin to walk, I am involved in the nuptial rite. The bride, as tradition demands, lives quite close to the church, and yet must travel that stretch without ever touching the ground, entrusting herself to a carriage harnessed with two horses, one white, the other black. So she will leave her home when I myself have been walking already for quite some time. Still it is not at all certain that the bride must proceed directly from her home to the temple. She has the right to follow streets that do not lead directly to her goal, and she can turn the last of her maiden mornings into a lengthy meander, no matter that it always must conclude in the church where our separate destinies will be welded into one.

I begin to walk as the city's vitality slowly swells up around me. My pace is unhurried since a great deal of time lies before me, and I know this span to be mutable and abstract: the time between two moments of ritual can never be measured exactly. Resignation is required, and I am very resigned. A beggar pleads politely that I halt, beseeching relief from an antique poverty. Perhaps my ceremonial dress has persuaded him that I am blessed with wealth; in any case I do not want to turn him away, and I proffer a perhaps incautious coin. Expressing his thanks, the beggar then briefly alluded to a personal history more unfortunate than unhappy: born to a decorous family, he had grown into a studious youth attentive to the dignity of a life devoted to the arts; he next referred to an error of the passions, adding that poverty was his payment for a happiness of which now he could measure the blasphemy, but which nonetheless he could not disown. I look at the beggar and realize I could make no estimate of his age; perhaps he is young, no older that I. I study his features carefully, and he faces me with an innocent, quiet gaze, offering a strangely affirmative nod, as though suggesting not only that he understands, but agrees with me as well. Yet on what he might agree, I have not the slightest idea. Impulsively, I ask him whether this is the road to the church, and after a pause, as though sifting through memories, he replies that, yes, of that there can be no doubt. He motions me to hasten, courteously releasing me with a bow, and I return to my path. This beggar caused no derangement of my calm contentment, though still he made me thoughtful. I wonder at his certainty that this is the street to the church, since this temple opens its portals only to a bride and groom, and no one else.

The first crossing enlarges into a circular plaza, with at its center a somewhat skimpy flowerbed around a monument to justice, cast as a massively awkward female figure. I stop to observe it more closely, and as I study the heavy opaque form, I am accosted by a dignified gentleman who asks if I might require the benefit of a credible description of the statue. Prior to any ability to reflect, I realize that my reply has been affirmative. But the time allotted for my ceremonial promenade, though difficult to measure, is virtually unlimited.

"What you here admire," the scholar began, "is a statue of Justice. The city takes proper pride in so ambitious a monument, from the ideological point of view. You will appreciate the scales," and then he pointed to this obvious, irritating image, "which stand for equity and rigor. Note as well the outsized flanks, expressing the certainty that justice is always undefiable—a place not only of stability, but truly a throne. The woman, as you doubtless remark, could not be said to be beautiful; and precisely for the reason that it is no task of Justice to display alluring features. Her features ought in fact to arouse a slight disgust. She flatters, loves, and recognizes no one. Her gaze, as you see, is distracted and vacant, for her interest turns only upon herself. Still her power is enormous, which is the power," the guide insisted, "not so much of Justice as concept, but of this statue itself, this very monument. Not many years ago, an aged man, already more than ninety, was taken as he stood here before this statue by a sudden rapture and confessed to two unpunished crimes of his distant youth. In thrall to sensual jealousy, he had taken the life of his closest friend; he had joined him on a tranquil country jaunt and then thrown him from a cliff into a dark abyss where he dissolved in a long and satisfying howl. The boy had also murdered an innocent chance witness, and later a melancholic gentleman who nourished a suspicion of his crimes. He had jettisoned all these corpses into the depths of that single gully, which he sited and described with exemplary clarity. Investigations were immediately undertaken but revealed no trace of such ancient crimes, as though the passage of time had cancelled them out, the murders never committed. The man could not be brought to trial and lapsed into a form of dementia. He insisted that the female form before you, Justice, would never permit that he die unpunished. He then spun tales of further crimes, purporting times and places and means that were savage and horrid—all of which homicides were patently false. Finally, it grew plain—whether or not he had ever committed any misdeed whatsoever—that a bond had fastened between the statue and the doddering old man and could only be appeased by an act of justice. A generous perjurer accused him of a spurious atrocity, and the criminal was condemned to hard sentence, to be served in absolute freedom and accompanied by a guaranteed wage. The aged culprit then lived for several years in an orgy of outrageous delight: the words of obscenity that you here make out, almost though not entirely cancelled by the years, these graffiti on the teats of justice are the work of none other than this aged, crime-riddled creature. It might be added that a skull was discovered a few years after his death. So it seems not fully impossible that indeed he did bear guilt for the crime that seemed no more than fatuous swagger. Justice, good sir, cannot forgive, and, lacking a reasonable crime to punish, will make accusal of another that is senseless. It is not, sir, that the crime begets Justice, but entirely the opposite: the crime is begotten by Justice. I hope that thoughts on this weighty, ill-shaped being will offer consolation as you continue along your way."

Perplexed and thoughtful, I returned to walking. A final glance had left no doubts about the strange similarity between the guide and the beggar. And that final phrase, half under his breath, had disturbed me: it seemed to caution me not halt along my path.

I walked on thoughtfully for a while, until I realized

I was not alone. Unawares, I had slowed my pace and fallen into step with a cortege dressed in mourning and trailing behind a funeral, modest but dignified. Someone directed me a nod of greeting, as though I were someone he would know, even family. I replied with measured gravity. Perhaps I was told the story, or so it seemed, of the man we were taking to his final home. A mediocre life, but hardly vile, tolerated with pointless patience; and slowly riddled by misadventure, sickness, moral decay, and the sordid vices of age: drink, gambling, the more miserly forms of sex. No one present seemed disturbed by the death, all of them exuding a sort of generic sadness: a profound disbelief in any possibility for a somehow decent funeral accompanied by a credible pain.

What was the hand that furtively slipped into mine, on the right, as I joined this cheerless cortege? I walk at the flank of a woman in widow's weeds, a woman with a joyless, strangely common face, a face perhaps dreamed. She briefly smiled in my direction, in a way that dealt no offense to the sadness of the occasion, and she lightly pressed my hand. Why did I acknowledge that touch? I know I am a groom on the way to his marriage, and yet I do not manage to censure behavior that strikes me as ambiguous, though perhaps I interpret it as more flattering than it is. Has she mistaken me for an acquaintance? But this, I have to admit, is unlikely, since the pressure of this hand in my own would not betoken a recent familiarity. She might, however, suppose me so grieved as to need some gesture of consolation! I turn to look at her, but she is no longer where she was; she is slightly at a distance, because a little girl walks between us, giving her right hand to me and the left to her. The funeral draws away from us, and something in our stride seems distracted, casual, and habitual. The air is mild, daily noises throng the street; I presume that this is the road to the church, but I am not sure, and I dare not ask the silent woman beside me about the direction in which we walk. When we enter a modest though not disreputable house—and I could not say whether I guided the way or was guided to it—I never question obedience to the strange imperative that controls me. Might it be forbidden for me to sit at this table with the strange, silent woman before me, or to take a bite with the two small children who are with us? I have a great deal of time, and must only be careful not to soil my suit. I smile at the woman who faces me and I am certain I have never sat with her before, nor met, nor seen her. She is not the woman at the funeral, nor the one with whom I walked. Have I done something wrong? No one seems to suppose that there is anything unseemly, yet I cannot avoid perceiving a mixture of happiness and discomfort, and I would like to make some gesture that would clear the air; I feel myself a coward, more than ever before.

I realize that a woman is beside me, standing, appearing nearly to await the end of a meal I have never begun, and that then I abandon that house. With a touch of anxiety I glance towards the woman who sits directly in front of me and now there is something I would like to explain. But I am ignorant of what actually is taking place. I can manage no more than a vacant nod of departure while rising from my seat. I walk, and again beside the figure of a woman. I lack the courage to look at her, but feel by now that a great deal of time, a very great deal, has already passed, and that further delay perhaps is impermissible. The ceremony is surely inclusive of many strange gestures, but I do not know if the occurences I have come to be involved in can be numbered among them. Is this the road? I turn towards the woman who flanks me and find that I am alone. The light is violet, as after many hours of weary wandering. Along the street, I see a few boys in dark suits, and they nod respectfully. For a moment I wonder if I am again caught up in a funeral, and I dare not ponder whose it might be. I turn sharply to approach the boys, but watch them draw back in fear. Behind them is a group of women dressed in black who cover the children's faces as though warding off the sight of something monstrous.

At a street corner, a beggar extends his hand. Have I backtracked along my course? Am I perhaps in a street that leads to no church, or only to the chapel of the dead? I study the beggar, who might be the same one as before, perhaps another. I approach him and he lifts his eyes. I remain perplexed. I cannot tell whether or not he is the same man, though to know is by now of the utmost importance. I withdraw a gold coin from my pocket, but he regards it with disinterest. Can it possibly be so late? Can I have changed so much that my gestures are totally useless? I ask him for directions to the street that leads to the church of the betrothed. He looks at me with amazed curiosity and nods that this is the street of the church of the betrothed. Something in his manner brings a flood of apprehension. But immediately I reconsider. In fact, I am standing before the very portal of the church of the betrothed, and the beggar could only have been astonished by such a lack of perception. How my pace now quickens! The calm delight of the morning has returned, and I seem to hold within my hand the destiny which I am now to unite irrevocably with another. I direct myself to the portal of the church with a hasty childlike glee!

The great doors stand fully open, I see the carpet that will lead the betrothed to the altar. But no one stands on the steps before the church, no one anywhere around it. The bridal carriage is nowhere in sight. Am I to imagine that my bride is yet to arrive? Reaching the very threshold of the church, I am amazed by the vision before me. Huge bouquets of flowers stand everywhere, but wilted; dry dead petals litter the floor. The candles have burned to stumps, and the few still aglow are about to gutter out. Have I arrived too late? Someone grasps my arm, and I turn to face the celebrant who has always officiated at our city's marriages. "Wretched creature," he begins, his voice hoarse with exhaustion though free from anger, as though he too had been the victim of some heinous catastrophe. "Wretched creature. Your bride is not here. Yet how often you have met her along the road! How many times you have dined and slept with her, how many children you have blessed with a father's affection! But not here! Never here! For two hundred years, your bride came daily in her carriage to await you: your bride, the woman with whom you traveled the whole of your road. But you come too late, far too late! Look at this ring!"—and he showed me a minuscule circle, gleaming like the golden coin I had given the beggar. Or had I given the beggar this ring itself? "Yesterday, and not a day sooner, your bride approached me in tears and handed me this ring, with the words: 'My groom has not come to the church, and now will never come; I can hold his hand in the crowds at funerals, I can dine with him in silence in a house not ours. My groom has been unfaithful.' Crying, and oh how she cried, she gave me this ring, and yesterday she forever departed, you wretched man, for another land, and she will never return to await you before this church!" As he spoke, I was invaded by a great, solemn, and wonderful pain. Now I know who slipped a hand into mine as I walked behind the funeral. I know that I was always destined never to reach the church, though never ceasing to encounter my bride. Kneeling on the threshold of the temple as its doors swing closed, I cry and shiver, and invoke my faithless bride.